FALSE WITNESS

ALSO BY PHILLIP MARGOLIN

Heartstone
The Last Innocent Man
Gone, But Not Forgotten
After Dark
The Burning Man
The Undertaker's Widow
The Associate
Sleeping Beauty
Lost Lake
Worthy Brown's Daughter
Woman with a Gun
Vanishing Acts (with Ami Margolin Rome)
An Insignificant Case

AMANDA JAFFE NOVELS
Wild Justice
Ties That Bind
Proof Positive
Fugitive
Violent Crimes

ROBIN LOCKWOOD NOVELS
The Third Victim
The Perfect Alibi
A Reasonable Doubt
A Matter of Life and Death
The Darkest Place
Murder at Black Oaks
Betrayal

DANA CUTLER NOVELS
Executive Privilege
Supreme Justice
Capitol Murder
Sleight of Hand

FALSE WITNESS

A NOVEL

PHILLIP MARGOLIN

MINOTAUR
BOOKS
NEW YORK

This is a work of fiction. All of the characters, organizations, and events portrayed in this novel are either products of the author's imagination or are used fictitiously.

First published in the United States by Minotaur Books, an imprint of St. Martin's Publishing Group

EU Representative: Macmillan Publishers Ireland Ltd, 1st Floor, The Liffey Trust Centre, 117–126 Sheriff Street Upper, Dublin 1, DO1 YC43

FALSE WITNESS. Copyright © 2025 by Phillip Margolin. All rights reserved. Printed in the United States of America. For information, address St. Martin's Publishing Group, 120 Broadway, New York, NY 10271.

www.minotaurbooks.com

Designed by Omar Chapa

The Library of Congress Cataloging-in-Publication Data is available upon request.

ISBN 978-1-250-35689-5 (hardcover)
ISBN 978-1-250-35690-1 (ebook)

The publisher of this book does not authorize the use or reproduction of any part of this book in any manner for the purpose of training artificial intelligence technologies or systems. The publisher of this book expressly reserves this book from the Text and Data Mining exception in accordance with Article 4(3) of the European Union Digital Single Market Directive 2019/790.

Our books may be purchased in bulk for specialty retail/wholesale, literacy, corporate/premium, educational, and subscription box use. Please contact MacmillanSpecialMarkets@macmillan.com.

First Edition: 2025

10 9 8 7 6 5 4 3 2 1

For Marlys Pierson and Don Girard, two of my oldest and dearest friends

FALSE WITNESS

PROLOGUE

Karen Wyatt had auburn hair, emerald eyes, high cheekbones, and a slender figure that had survived one year of the unhealthy food she was served at the Coffee Creek Correctional Facility, Oregon's women's prison. Dressed in the navy-blue jacket and skirt and cream-colored blouse she had changed into before leaving the prison, Karen looked like the lawyer she had been before she was convicted of a felony, sentenced to prison, and disbarred.

Harry Schmidt, Karen's attorney, was waiting for his client when she got out of the van that had transported Karen to the courthouse. Schmidt, the senior partner in one of Portland's best firms, was forty-two, but a head of premature white hair made him look older and, he hoped, wiser. Harry noticed the angry stares that the guards cast at Karen when she got out of the van. One of the guards grabbed Karen's elbow and jerked her forward. Harry started to say something but stopped himself. There were a lot of people in law enforcement who hated his client, and he wasn't going to change this guard's mind, no matter what he said. What he could do was make sure that Karen didn't make a return trip to the prison.

"Good morning, Counselor," Harry said.

Karen smiled. It had been a long time since anyone had addressed her as if she were an attorney.

"Is it going to be good?" Karen asked.

"You bet it will," Harry said. "See you in court."

"Get moving," the guard barked as she shoved Karen forward. Harry had had enough.

"Listen to me, asshole. My client is going to be a free woman and a practicing member of the bar by the end of the day. That means that she will be able to sue you into oblivion if you ruffle so much as one hair on her head. So treat her with respect if you want to avoid bankruptcy and a charge of assault and battery."

The guard glared at Harry, but she held her tongue. Harry noticed that the guard didn't touch Karen anymore as she took her into the courthouse and up to the jail, where Karen would have to wait until her case was called.

Harry walked back inside the courthouse and rode the elevator up to the courtroom where Karen's post-conviction case was being tried. A herd of reporters stampeded toward Harry when he walked down the corridor. They bombarded him with questions, which he fended off with the skill of an Olympic fencer. Harry had tried to keep the post-conviction hearing under the radar so Karen would be able to start her new life with a minimum of commotion, but there was no way that this bombshell could be kept under wraps. The courtroom was packed with reporters, members of the district attorney's office, and the public.

Harry walked through the bar of the court and nodded to Muriel Lujack, the deputy district attorney who had been assigned to defend the State of Oregon. Lujack was a new hire, and Harry had never met her. She nodded back quickly, and Harry could see that she was very uncomfortable. He wasn't surprised. Everyone in the district attorney's office knew what was going to happen this morning.

Moments after Harry was seated, the bailiff signaled the guards to bring Karen to the courtroom. Lujack cast a quick look at Harry's client. When Karen met her eye, the deputy DA's cheeks flushed and she looked down at her notes to hide her embarrassment.

"How are you holding up?" Harry asked.

"I'm doing just fine," Karen said just as the door to the Honorable Teresa Herrera's chambers opened and she took her place on the bench.

"Good morning, Counselors. We are in court on a post-conviction case brought on behalf of Karen Wyatt. Is everyone ready to proceed?"

"We are," Harry and Muriel said.

"I understand that you have one witness, Mr. Schmidt," the judge said.

"I do. Miss Wyatt calls Garrett Loman to the stand."

The door to the area where prisoners were held opened, and a middle-aged man with curly gray hair, downcast blue eyes, and a sallow complexion walked out. He took a quick look at the spectator section. Then he looked down at the floor as he walked to the witness stand.

Harry checked his notes while the witness swore an oath to tell the truth. When Loman was seated, Harry looked him in the eye. Loman tried to keep eye contact, but he didn't have the heart to continue the staring contest and he looked away.

"Mr. Loman," Harry said, "how were you employed before

you were convicted for stealing cocaine from the evidence locker at the Oregon State Crime Lab?"

"I was a forensic expert employed by the Oregon State Crime Lab."

"A sworn officer of the law?" Schmidt asked.

"Yes."

"Please tell Judge Herrera how you violated your oath when you testified in Miss Wyatt's trial."

"I . . ." Loman paused and licked his lips. Then he took a drink of water. "I lied at her trial. I said that I dusted a package containing a kilo of cocaine that had been found during a search of Miss Wyatt's apartment and found her prints on it."

"Were her prints on the baggie?"

"No."

"Without going into the details of how you did it, did you manufacture the prints that you swore were Miss Wyatt's?"

"Yes."

"Please tell the judge why you did this."

Loman took another sip of water. Then he answered without looking at the judge. His voice was strained, and he looked sick.

"I left work one night. A policeman was waiting by my car."

"What was the officer's name?"

"Max Ellis."

"Go on."

"He said that he knew I was an addict and had been stealing cocaine from the evidence that I was supposed to be testing. He said that he would go to the district attorney if I didn't plant your client's prints on a package containing cocaine that was going to be found in Miss Wyatt's apartment and then testify in court that I had found her prints on the package."

"Did you learn anything else about the plot to frame Miss Wyatt?"

"Ellis arrested Julio Cortez. He was a drug dealer. Cortez provided the basis for a search warrant. He said he'd sold the cocaine to Miss Wyatt."

"What happened to Mr. Cortez's case?"

"Ellis told me to get rid of the evidence in it. When I did, it was dismissed."

"What happened when the search warrant was executed?"

"Officer Ellis was working Narcotics and participated in the search. He's the one who said he'd found the cocaine."

"Why did you expose this plot against Miss Wyatt?"

"One of the people I worked with discovered that I had a habit and was stealing cocaine from evidence. He told the DA, and I was arrested. My attorney made a deal for me. I'll get probation if I tell the truth about the plot to frame your client."

"Why aren't Mr. Ellis and Mr. Cortez testifying today?"

"Mr. Cortez was murdered a week after the search, and Officer Ellis was murdered a few days after I made the deal with the DA."

"Why haven't you been killed?"

"I'm in a witness protection program."

"Do you know why Miss Wyatt was framed?"

"I asked Officer Ellis why he was doing this. He said they were going . . . These were his words, not mine. He said they were going to teach the bitch what happened to someone who ratted out a cop."

"Do you know what he was referring to?"

"Miss Wyatt represented a biker who was charged with assaulting a police officer during a raid on the biker gang's clubhouse. She won an acquittal by proving that her client acted in self-defense. During the trial, she introduced evidence that showed that the raid was planned by a district attorney and police officers who were being bribed by a rival biker gang. The DA and several officers were sent to prison. It was a big scandal."

"Do you have any idea who else was involved in framing Miss Wyatt?"

"No."

"No further questions, Your Honor," Karen's lawyer said.

"Miss Lujack?" Judge Herrera asked the prosecutor.

Muriel Lujack looked uncomfortable, which was to be expected, since she'd only been a deputy DA for six months and the hearing was exposing corruption in the police force and her office.

Karen had expected to see Oscar Vanderlasky at the prosecution table. He was the DA who had tried the case that sent her to prison. She guessed that Vanderlasky didn't have the guts to face her, and she assumed that Muriel Lujack had been assigned to represent the State at this hearing because no one else in the office wanted to be embarrassed.

"No questions," Lujack said.

"Any more witnesses, Mr. Schmidt?"

"No, Your Honor."

"Unless you or Miss Lujack want to present an argument, I'm ready to rule on the motion to set aside Miss Wyatt's conviction."

"I'll defer to the court," Schmidt said.

"I don't have anything to say," the prosecutor answered. She looked ashamed.

The judge turned to Karen. "Miss Wyatt, I cannot imagine the hell you've been through these past years. What happened to you . . . Well, I have no words to describe it. I will cut to the chase. I am vacating your conviction and ordering your immediate release. Additionally, as soon as court is in recess, I am going to call the Oregon State Bar and recommend that you be reinstated immediately."

The judge turned to the prosecutor. "Miss Lujack, do you intend to appeal my decision?"

"No, Your Honor. Our office was shocked by what we learned. I can only wish Miss Wyatt the best."

"I join in Miss Lujack's statement. Please call me if there is anything I can do to help you."

Judge Herrera left the bench. Karen leaned her head back and closed her eyes. Then she took a deep breath and opened them. There were no tears.

"Thank you, Harry," she said.

"*Thank you* for letting me do a good deed I will keep remembering whenever the practice of law gets me down."

"You took this case pro bono, but we are going to sue everyone I can think of. When you get me my settlement, name your fee, and I'll pay it."

"I will never charge you for this case." Harry smiled. "Of course, I do anticipate a very fat payout when we conclude your lawsuit."

Karen laughed.

"You don't seem bitter," Harry said.

"I'm not. I'm angry. I want to find the people who did this to me. Then I want those motherfuckers sent to a deep, dark place."

"Do you have any leads?"

"Not really. I've been too preoccupied with survival for the past year to do much investigating."

"Do you want to speak to the reporters? They'll be waiting to ambush you when you step into the hall."

"I'm not afraid of the press. In fact, I'm going to ask them to help me find the people who framed me. They'll love getting a juicy investigative assignment."

"Prison hasn't changed you much. You're still the feisty young attorney who kicked my butt the only time we faced off."

Karen laughed. "You didn't have much of a case."

Harry smiled. "That's not what I thought before the trial started." He stood up. "Shall we face the Fourth Estate?"

"Let's," Karen said. She stood and straightened her skirt.

"Miss Wyatt."

Karen turned and found herself face-to-face with Morris Johnson, the detective who had arrested her for cocaine possession. Johnson was in his midthirties with curly black hair, brown eyes, and the beginning of a paunch. He had been courteous when he arrested her, and Karen had the impression that he hadn't enjoyed taking her into custody.

"I wanted to tell you how sorry I am for what you've gone through," Johnson said.

"Thank you for coming and looking me in the eye, but I don't see anyone else from the Portland PB here."

"You won't. They're closing ranks. This scandal has everyone looking over their shoulder."

Karen nodded. "I'm not surprised. Now, I have to meet the press."

"Good luck," Johnson said as he stepped aside to let Karen pass. She straightened her shoulders and strode toward the courtroom door. Johnson didn't think she looked like a victim. He thought she looked like a warrior.

PART ONE

UNIDENTIFIED FLYING OBJECTS

THREE YEARS LATER

CHAPTER ONE

The hearing room in the United States House of Representatives was standing room only, because the American public wanted to know if flying saucers and little green men from another planet were the real deal. United States representative Thomas Horan was one of the few people in the room who didn't care if an alien invasion were imminent. He was only interested in making the six o'clock news.

The congressman was barely five foot, three inches tall. Even though he was only in his midthirties, he had lost a majority of his hair and his belly overlapped his belt. Horan had gone through life with a massive chip on his shoulder as a result of being bullied in every stage of his public school education.

The congressman was very intelligent and had found success in high school on the chess team, but he'd had little success with girls. It wasn't until he got involved in campus politics in college that he got laid for the first time and found his calling.

Margo Sparks, an ex-CIA agent, was leading a crusade to prove that the government was covering up the fact that aliens in flying saucers had visited the earth. Horan had been champing at the bit for his chance to question Sparks. He was facing a tough opponent in the next election, and he would be the recipient of publicity that money could not buy if he could perform a star turn when his chance to examine Sparks arrived.

"Mrs. Sparks," Horan said when the committee chairman called his name, "you have claimed that there are numerous credible sightings of flying objects with abilities that no earthly aircraft can duplicate."

"There are, in fact, countless reports by reputable individuals—air force pilots, pilots in commercial aircrafts—of flying objects whose mechanical abilities can only be ascribed to alien technology."

"You also claim that your investigations have led you to conclude that one or more of these UFOs have crashed on Earth and that our government is hiding these crafts and the biological remains of their alien pilots."

"Yes. That's true."

Horan smiled at the ex–intelligence officer. "I must admit that you've got me all excited. Can you tell this committee and the American people what these aliens look like? Are they little green men?"

"I have not seen the wreckage or the alien remains personally."

"Do you have photos?"

"No. I haven't seen any of the alien crafts that the government has in storage, but more than three dozen reputable witnesses, who have seen the crafts, have assured me that they do exist."

"Great. Can you make me a list of these witnesses so I can subpoena them?"

"That information is classified."

"I see. Has our government talked to aliens?"

"I really can't discuss that. The information is classified."

"So, you have never seen an alien body?"

"No, but people who have assure me that they have been recovered at crash sites."

"If there are so many witnesses who have actually seen aliens and their crafts, why haven't you brought any of them to this hearing?"

"These people are threatened with retaliation if they go public."

"What type of retaliation?"

"Loss of jobs, public humiliation, and physical threats."

"You're saying that you know people who have been injured physically to cover up the existence of UFOs?"

"Yes."

"Has anyone ever been murdered as part of this cover-up?"

"I can't comment on that."

Horan sighed and shook his head. "Mrs. Sparks, you've made a lot of outrageous claims, but am I right in concluding that you have not supplied one single piece of concrete evidence to this committee—like a photo or a person who has seen these aliens and their crafts—that proves that our government is hiding alien spacecrafts and alien corpses?"

"I can't supply this information in a public forum."

"That's because you don't have any evidence to supply. Quite frankly, Mrs. Sparks, you are full of hot air, and the reason you can't prove your assertion is that alien abductions, UFOs from other planets, and the existence of little green men are science fiction and not science fact. I have no further questions, Mr. Chairman."

When Thomas Horan deplaned at Portland International Airport, Julie Sunderland, his campaign manager, was waiting with crews from the television networks and reporters from several Oregon newspapers. Standing with Julie was Francine Horan, Thomas's wife, who had handled PR for the congressman before marrying him and knew just what to do when her husband walked toward the reporters.

Francine left Sunderland's side and walked into her husband's waiting arms.

"How did I do, honey?" Thomas asked as the cameras recorded the conquering hero being welcomed by his adoring wife.

"You knocked the ball out of the park," Francine said, loudly enough for the reporters to hear her.

"That's what I want to hear," Horan said before pivoting and smiling for the cameras.

For the next fifteen minutes, Horan answered questions. Then Julie stepped in.

"The congressman is exhausted from his cross-country flight. So, why don't we get one more question and call it a day?"

Julie pointed at a reporter from *The Oregonian*. "Lacey?"

"Do you think that the hearing uncovered any evidence that ETs have visited Earth in flying saucers?"

"I think that the witnesses who testified that they have were misguided, and I can't think of one piece of concrete evidence that supports a conclusion that we have been visited by aliens from other planets."

Horan started walking toward the exit.

"Thank you for coming out, but, as Julie said, these cross-country flights are exhausting, and I have to get home for my first home-cooked meal in several weeks."

Horan thanked Sunderland for rounding up the reporters and told her he'd see her in the morning. As soon as he and Francine were in the car, Horan closed his eyes and put his head back.

"You were great, Tom," Francine said as she drove out of the lot and onto the highway.

"Yeah, I thought I nailed it."

"I bought a steak and a great pinot to celebrate."

Horan opened his eyes and smiled. "You're the best. I'll take a quick shower. Then we'll eat, and later . . ." He winked.

Francine laughed. "What would the voters say if they knew I was married to a sex maniac?"

"Anyone married to you wouldn't be able to think about anything all day but making love."

The steak was great and the wine was superb, and Thomas was almost finished with his meal when his cell phone rang. He checked the caller ID and stood up.

"I've got to take this," he apologized.

"Go ahead. I'll clear the table."

Horan went into the living room, and Francine couldn't hear what he was saying. A few minutes later, when he walked back to the dining room, Horan looked upset.

"I've got to go out."

"Do you have to? You just got home."

"Sorry. It's important. I should be back soon."

Francine looked disappointed. Horan kissed her. Then he grabbed his jacket and walked out of the house.

CHAPTER TWO

If Portland detective Chad Remington's partner, Audrey Packer, was an inanimate object, Remington imagined that she would be a wire. Packer was strung tight and she had a slender, wiry physique that was the product of years practicing Brazilian jujitsu, a martial art in which she held a black belt.

If Audrey Packer engaged in the same mental exercise, she would probably imagine that Remington was a sofa. It wasn't that he was soft. Chad still had the large, solid build of the linebacker he'd been at Oregon State. But he was a comfortable, easygoing counterpoint to Packer's intensity.

Packer had been complaining constantly during the drive to Congressman Horan's house.

"We're Homicide. Why are we working this case?"

"We are working this case because the DA called our boss and our boss told us to get our asses to Horan's house to see what we could see."

"Fucking politics," Audrey swore.

"Horan is a member of the United States Congress and is one of the DA's biggest donors," Remington reminded his partner.

"That's what I just said: 'Fucking politics.' Horan has only been missing two days. He's probably shacked up with one of his interns."

"Quit complaining and put on a happy face so we don't get a bad Yelp review," Remington said as he parked in front of a yellow Dutch colonial with white trim that was set back on a large lot in Portland's West Hills.

Moments after Packer rang the bell, the front door opened and the detectives found themselves face-to-face with Francine Horan, the woman the congressman had married after the conclusion of his highly publicized and contentious divorce from his college sweetheart, Millie Horan. The reason for the divorce was the congressman's affair with Francine, who handled his public relations and who had been involved in intimate relations with Horan while the representative was three thousand miles away from Millie in Washington, DC.

Millie had come out of the divorce with a lot of money after she'd agreed to sign a nondisclosure agreement. There had been rumors that she would have been able to disclose a lot of tasty information about the source of the congressman's finances.

Audrey and Chad held up their credentials. Francine barely looked at them before inviting the detectives into a large living room. Remington could see why the congressman had been attracted to his new wife. Francine was blond and slender with the large breasts and narrow waist Remington imagined

Horan had fantasized about when he was watching internet porn during his virginal days in high school. The difference between the internet blondes and Horan's wife was the absence of a winsome smile on their host's face. Instead, Remington saw the drawn, exhausted look of someone who had not had a restful sleep.

Francine sat in a large armchair, and the detectives sat side by side on a couch across from her.

"Can I get you coffee or tea?" Francine asked.

"We're good," Chad answered with a smile that he hoped would relax Horan's wife.

"Thank you for coming so quickly," Francine said.

"When was the last time you saw your husband?" asked Packer, who was not a fan of small talk.

"He flew back from DC after the UFO hearing two days ago. I picked him up at the airport, and we drove home. Then he got a call. He didn't say who was calling. After he hung up, Tom said that he would be home soon. He wasn't home by the time I went to bed, so I called his phone. The call went to voicemail. Then he wasn't home in the morning. That's when I thought he might have been in an accident, and I called Frank," she said, referring to Frank Curtin, the newly elected Multnomah County district attorney. "He told me to wait a day. Tom didn't come home last night, so I called first thing."

"What do you think happened to your husband?" Chad asked.

"I have no idea. He's never done anything like this before."

"Have you tried his phone again?" Chad asked.

"He doesn't answer."

"Okay. We'll get on it. We can call hospitals, check to see if he was in an accident," Chad said. "We'll also need the names and addresses of anyone he might have gone to visit."

When Remington and Packer finished their interview with Mrs. Horan, they headed back to the precinct. On the way, the dispatcher told them that Congressman Horan's car had been found on a side road near a farm in rural Silverton.

CHAPTER THREE

Karen Wyatt walked into her penthouse and placed the takeout order of pad thai on the kitchen counter. Her license to practice law had been restored shortly after Harry Schmidt had cleared her name. In the three years since she had restarted her practice, the publicity from her case had drawn enough clients that she had been forced to hire three associates. Karen was thrilled to be practicing law again, but after a day in court with Oscar Vanderlasky, a candidate for the Idiots' Hall of Fame, she had started thinking of a new career as a travel agent or dog walker. Karen sighed. The trial would be over soon, and she was going to win. She didn't have another case scheduled for court until next month. She would survive.

Karen fixed her dinner. Vanderlasky would start calling witnesses in the morning. She was tempted to review her notes when she finished eating, but she knew she was thoroughly prepared and she decided to relax with a romantic comedy on Netflix. By the time the movie ended, she could barely keep her eyes open. Fifteen minutes later, she was in bed, and soon after she pulled the covers up, she was in a deep sleep.

The nightmare wasn't new. It was one of several with a recurring theme that she had experienced periodically since she had been released from prison. Sometimes she was a bird in a cage who beat its wings against the bars in a futile effort to get out. This night, Karen was a child who was trapped in a closet that no light penetrated. She pounded her little fist against the door, she screamed for help. No one came, and the walls seemed to be closing in. She couldn't breathe, and that's when she shot up in bed, her heart pounding.

It didn't take a Sigmund Freud to figure out the origin of Karen's nightmare. Spending a year in prison for a crime you didn't commit would play havoc with anyone's psyche. The experience left scars that could cripple a person, unless she believed Nietzsche's proposition that things that don't kill us make us stronger. Karen embraced that assertion.

She wanted to rest in her bed to recover from her nightmare, but she couldn't relax. She walked into her kitchen and poured ice water from the filter in her refrigerator into a tall glass. She carried the glass into the spacious living room of the $2 million penthouse she'd purchased with a small part of the multimillion-dollar settlement Harry Schmidt had gotten her. Harry didn't have to work too hard to get the city to cave. He sensed that everyone Karen was suing wanted her sordid tale buried and forgotten.

The main reason Karen had purchased this penthouse was the large living room with its floor-to-ceiling windows that provided a view across the Willamette River to the snow-covered slopes of majestic Mount Hood. After a year shut up between the concrete walls of a tiny cell with no view of the sky or stars, she needed these constant reminders that she was a free woman.

Karen looked out at the lights that illuminated Portland. There was a full moon and enough stars to make the sky look like a tapestry that celebrated the majesty of the universe. She savored the view while she finished the water in her glass. By the time the glass was empty, she had relaxed enough to believe she would be able to sleep. She returned to the bedroom and got between the covers. Then she turned off the light on her nightstand, hopeful that she would get the rest she needed to be fit enough to eviscerate the case Oscar Vanderlasky was going to present to a jury in the morning.

For many years, the Multnomah County Courthouse had been an eight-story, gray concrete building that occupied a block in the middle of downtown Portland. The courthouse had been constructed between 1909 and 1914, and it had been abandoned in 2020 after a new, modern, seismically safer building was constructed near the west end of the Hawthorne Bridge. The new location gave visitors and the courthouse staff a view of boats cruising the Willamette River and the majestic snow-covered slopes of the Cascade Mountain Range.

The courtrooms in the old courthouse featured high ceilings, ornate molding, marble Corinthian columns, and daises of polished wood. The courtrooms in the new building had none of the grandeur or historic character of the old courtrooms. They had flat, dull, brown wooden desks with clean lines that could have been bought at IKEA and were built for function, not form. Attorneys could charge laptops or phones in outlets in their counsel tables. Videos and evidence were presented to jurors on wall-mounted screens.

Deputy district attorneys Oscar Vanderlasky and Muriel Lujack were already seated at the counsel table closest to the jury box when Karen entered Judge Leo Cohen's courtroom with her client, Laurie Post.

Many DAs would have refused to charge Post, the victim of an abusive boyfriend. Vanderlasky had gleefully prosecuted Post as soon as he learned that Karen was representing her. He was part of a group of prosecutors and police officers who tried to make Karen's life miserable ever since she had exposed corruption in the police force and DA's office. Karen had always wondered if Vanderlasky was involved in the frame that had sent her to prison.

If Karen had looked up *WASP* in the dictionary, she wouldn't have been surprised to see a picture of the square-jawed, blue-eyed, blond Vanderlasky attired in a blazer and school tie. The pompous prosecutor had gone to Stanford on a tennis scholarship, where he had excelled on the court and received mediocre grades in class. His parents, alumni and major donors at the University of Oregon, had pulled strings to get him admitted to the law school, where he had finished near the bottom of his class.

Vanderlasky was an egotist who thought he was a genius and blamed his failures on everyone but himself. In fact, he was not very bright, and he was lazy and sloppy when he prepared a case. Karen was counting on these character traits. If Vanderlasky was true to form, he was sure to have overlooked the significance of the fact that the lamp in Laurie Post's living room was not plugged into the wall socket when the police arrived at her apartment.

Muriel Lujack was a stark contrast to Vanderlasky, who had a sliding scale when it came to moral issues, assuming that he even thought about right and wrong. The young prosecutor viewed moral issues as black and white and was as severe in her dress as she was in her view of good and evil. From a distance, Muriel could be mistaken for a nun. Her everyday attire was a black jacket, a straight black skirt that reached her ankles, and a white blouse that buttoned at the neck. Muriel's straight, black hair fell to her shoulders and she used the bare minimum of makeup. The young prosecutor was so thin that some people suspected that she was anorexic. The truth was that Lujack had no interest in food and felt that time eating was time wasted when she could be working on her cases.

In a lengthy stretch of her strict Catholic upbringing, Muriel had seriously considered joining a convent, but she had changed her career goal in her last year of parochial school when she decided that she could best combat evil and protect the good by prosecuting criminals.

Yesterday, a jury had been impaneled to hear Laurie Post's case. After Karen and Vanderlasky made their opening statements, the prosecutor had called the EMTs who had responded to Laurie's 911 call and the police officers who had arrived at the scene. Vanderlasky's last witness had been a doctor who testified that Ian Mowry, Post's boyfriend, had lost sight in his left eye and sustained a blow to his forehead that was consistent with being struck by a thick brass lamp that both sides had stipulated had been used to strike Mowry. During Karen's cross-examination, the doctor agreed that the blow could have been received when Mowry was sitting on the ground, if the blow had been delivered by a woman who was a little over five feet tall.

Judge Cohen's bailiff signaled the judge that the parties were in the courtroom. The judge took his place on the bench. Moments later, the jurors filed in and took their seats in the jury box. Karen watched them and was pleased to note that several jurors looked at her client and smiled.

"Call your first witness," Judge Cohen told the prosecutor.

"The State calls Ian Mowry," Vanderlasky said.

The door to the hall opened and the witness walked in. Mowry, a bodybuilder, was wearing a black eye patch and a tight shirt that showed off his narrow waist and massive chest. Karen felt that he would look right at home at a professional wrestling arena.

Mowry took the oath, then sat down in the witness-box.

"Mr. Mowry, what is your profession?" the DA asked.

"I'm a bus driver."

"Are you working as a bus driver right now?"

"No."

"Why is that?"

Mowry glared at Laurie Post. "She put my eye out. I can't drive with one eye."

"By 'she,' do you mean the defendant?"

"Yeah."

"How did that happen?"

"Me and the defendant was arguing. She got out of control and hit me with the lamp."

"State's Exhibit Five?"

"Yes, sir."

"Go on."

"Well, it stunned me, and I sat down. And that's when she stabbed me in the eye with her finger."

"I imagine that must have been horribly painful."

"I was screaming my head off and rolling around on the floor. There was blood all over."

"What have the doctors told you about regaining the sight in your eye?"

"They said it ain't gonna happen. It's permanent."

Vanderlasky turned his head toward Karen so the jurors wouldn't be able to see his face, and smirked.

"No further questions, Your Honor."

"Miss Wyatt?" Judge Cohen said.

"Thank you, Judge. Will you please stand up, Mr. Mowry?"

Mowry stood up.

"How tall are you?"

"Six-five."

Karen motioned Laurie to stand. "How tall is Miss Post?"

"I don't know. Five-two, five-three."

"So, you're a lot taller than Miss Post."

"That's obvious."

"If I told you that she weighs one hundred and six pounds, would that seem right?"

"I guess."

"How much do you weigh?"

"Around two fifty."

"Do you have a drinking problem?"

"No."

"You told the jury that you're not driving a bus because you lost the sight in your left eye."

"That's right."

"Isn't it true that you were fired for being drunk while driving your bus the day before the incident with Miss Post?"

"I wasn't drunk."

"So, you disagree with the riders who called 911 to report you to the police and the officer who stopped your bus and took you into custody for driving your bus while under the influence of alcohol?"

"I pled not guilty. I wasn't drunk."

"Who is Peter Chang, Mr. Mowry?"

"My supervisor."

"Is he the person who fired you for being drunk on the job?"

"He had no right to do that. I didn't get a hearing to give my side."

"Let's discuss how you lost the sight in your eye and suffered the blow to your head. You said that you and Miss Post were arguing."

"Yeah."

"Were you drinking because you felt sorry for yourself as a result of being fired?"

"I'd had a few, but I wasn't drunk."

"Did you blame Miss Post for getting you fired?"

"She didn't support me. She wasn't sympathetic."

"She bailed you out of jail, didn't she?"

"Yeah."

"Let's talk about what happened in Miss Post's apartment. It is her apartment, isn't it?"

"Yeah."

"Do you pay rent there?"

"No."

"But you're living there?"

"Yeah. She asked me to move in."

"Did she ask, or did you tell her you needed to move in because you'd been kicked out of the apartment you were renting?"

"I wasn't kicked out. Me and the landlord had a disagreement, and I asked Laurie . . . the defendant if I could move in while I looked for another place."

"Let's move on to the night of the incident. Didn't the argument between you and Miss Post start when Miss Post asked you to leave her apartment because you were drinking and getting abusive?"

"No."

"Mr. Mowry, you claim that Miss Post hit you with the lamp, then poked you in the eye."

"*Stabbed* me in the eye with her fingernail."

"I stand corrected. So, as I understand it, first, she stunned you by hitting you with the lamp, then, second, she stabbed you in the eye when you were on the floor."

"That's right."

"Didn't the action occur the other way around? Didn't she stab you in the eye first, because you were strangling her? Then hit you with the lamp when you threatened to kill her?"

"That's bull—" Mowry caught himself. "That's not how it happened."

Karen gave the bailiff several photographs and asked that they be marked as exhibits.

"I'm handing Mr. Mowry the photographs of Mr. Mowry's and Miss Post's injuries that were taken by the officers who arrived at the scene."

Karen held up a picture. "In this photograph, you're sitting on the floor across the room from the end table on which the lamp was originally standing."

"Yeah. She knocked me down with the lamp."

"Why didn't you stop her?"

"She surprised me."

"Can you see the base of the lamp in this picture?"

"Yes."

"There's a long cord with prongs at one end that you use to plug the lamp into the wall, isn't there?"

"Yeah."

"Is the lamp plugged into the wall socket?"

"No."

"Could she have hit you with the lamp while you were on the ground if the lamp was plugged in?"

Mowry hesitated. "No," he said after a moment.

"That's because it wouldn't reach, right?"

"Yeah."

"The lamp was plugged into the wall before Miss Post grabbed it to hit you, wasn't it?"

"Yeah."

"You look very well built. Do you work out a lot?"

"Right after I get off work."

"You played football and basketball in high school, didn't you?"

"Yeah."

"Do you have pretty good reflexes?"

"Yeah."

"I'm confused, Mr. Mowry. You're an athlete who outweighs Miss Post by about one hundred and fifty pounds, and you're a foot taller. Why didn't you knock the lamp away to keep from being hit?"

"I told you. She surprised me."

"That's what's confusing me. To get the lamp to hit you, Miss Post would have to go around the end table and unplug it. That would have given you a lot of time to prevent her from using it, wouldn't it?"

"I . . . I know what happened."

"Take a look at the photos of Miss Post's injuries. Aren't there bruises on her neck that are the type that would be there if someone was choking her? And isn't her lip split and her eye swollen shut?"

"So?"

"Miss Post told the officers that she jabbed you in the eye to keep you from strangling her. Wouldn't it make more sense that she stabbed you in the eye when you were close and face-to-face than if you were sitting on the floor?"

"I know what happened," Mowry insisted.

"Dr. Pitofsky testified that the blow to your head was consistent with a downward strike. Doesn't it make more sense that you were seated on the floor when Miss Post hit you with the lamp because you're so much taller than she is?"

"She hit me with the lamp before she poked out my eye."

"Miss Post told the officers that you dropped to the floor and started screaming that you were going to kill her because she stabbed you in the eye. When you started to struggle to your feet, she said that she unplugged the lamp and hit you to protect herself. Isn't that what happened?"

"No."

Karen turned to the judge. "I'm through with this witness."

The State rested, Karen made a series of legal motions, and the judge recessed for lunch. When the trial resumed at one thirty, Karen's first witness was the rider who called 911 to complain that Mowry was driving his bus while he was drunk. Then she called Peter Chang, Mowry's supervisor, and the officer who arrested Mowry for driving under the influence. Laurie Post was great during her direct examination, and Oscar Vanderlasky's cross was inept and ineffectual. It was closing in on three o'clock when Karen and Vanderlasky gave their closing arguments and the judge gave the jury instructions.

Judge Cohen sent the jury out and told the lawyers to make sure that his bailiff had their phone numbers. Mowry had been sitting in court and he glared at Karen and her client when they walked past him and went into the hall.

"How long do you think it will take the jury to decide?" Laurie asked.

Karen had a very good feeling for the way the case had gone, but she knew better than to get her client's hopes up.

"I never try to predict anything a jury will do," Karen said. "But I think we should hang around for a bit."

Karen's gut instinct proved accurate. Twenty minutes after the jurors retired to the jury room, the bailiff let the parties know that they had a verdict. Karen's gut tightened. The worst part of any trial was the time between knowing that the jury had reached a verdict and finding out what that verdict was.

The jury filed in when the parties were seated. None of the jurors looked at Laurie Post, and suddenly, Karen wasn't so sure of the result.

"Has the jury reached a verdict?" Judge Cohen asked.

A middle-aged woman who taught middle school stood up.

"Are you the foreperson, Mrs. Mackey?"

"Yes, sir."

"Will you read the verdict?"

The woman nodded. Karen held her breath while Mrs. Mackey read the boilerplate and let it out when she said the words *not guilty*. Laurie Post sagged in her seat, and Karen wrapped an arm around her shoulder.

Karen took a quick look across the aisle. Oscar Vanderlasky looked furious. The judge asked the parties if they wanted the jurors polled. Karen said she didn't. Oscar Vanderlasky insisted that each juror reveal their vote. It was unanimous. The judge dismissed the jury and called the court into recess.

Karen had been worried that Ian Mowry might go after her client, so she'd alerted the court guards. She didn't have to worry. As soon as the judge ended the court session, Mowry started berating Oscar Vanderlasky, and Karen and her client were able to slip out of the courtroom unmolested.

CHAPTER FOUR

Karen said goodbye to her grateful client. Then she headed back to her office, which occupied half of the tenth floor of a modern glass-and-steel high-rise a few blocks from Pioneer Courthouse Square, the heart of downtown Portland. She could afford the rent because she became independently wealthy when the city finally settled her civil suit. They say that money can't buy happiness, and that is true. But money did buy Karen her penthouse, her office, and the freedom to take the cases she wanted to handle. Her specialty was criminal law, but she had brought on experienced attorneys who were experts in personal injury law and family law. Her only rule when an associate was deciding whether to take a case was that they be on the right side of the issue. Since money was not a factor in deciding who the firm would represent, they didn't represent abusers in divorces, and they made sure that the injuries in personal injury cases were legit.

Karen's receptionist looked at her expectantly when she walked into the waiting room.

Karen smiled and gave a thumbs-up. "It was unanimous!"

The receptionist pumped her fist.

"Any calls I have to make?" Karen asked.

"It's been really quiet."

"Is Morris in?"

"He got back from talking to those witnesses on the coast an hour ago."

Shortly after she was reinstated in the bar, Karen Wyatt had been appointed to represent a client in a complicated case. Morris Johnson had been the lead detective, and her client had been convicted because of Johnson's brilliant investigation. Karen had been so impressed that she started asking around about Johnson and learned that he was an excellent detective who had been passed over for promotion and ostracized because of his support for her.

When Harry Schmidt negotiated the settlement that made her a multimillionaire, she asked Johnson if he would be willing to leave the Portland Police Bureau to become her investigator at three times the salary he was making as a detective. Johnson had accepted.

Morris Johnson's hobby was photography. The hall that led to the investigator's office was decorated with photographs of Haystack Rock, Multnomah Falls, Mount Hood, and other photographs of Oregon's natural wonders that Morris had taken.

Karen's investigator was typing a summary of his interviews on the coast when Karen walked in. He looked up.

"Unanimous not guilty!"

Morris beamed. "Way to go."

"I couldn't have done it without your excellent investigative skills."

"Hey, it takes two to tango, Miss Wyatt."

"And it takes a village to get an innocent person out of the clutches of the law when the law is represented by Oscar Vanderlasky."

Morris laughed. "Did he miss the importance of the lamp?"

"Of course he did." Karen shook her head. "He's an obnoxious twit, but I love trying cases against him because I know he will screw up. So, how is O'Reilly looking?" she asked.

Morris stopped smiling. "Not as good as we thought it was. I talked to the clerk, and he's not as positive about the ID as he was when he talked to the police, which is good. But the customer is dead certain O'Reilly robbed the store."

Karen sighed. "You can't win 'em all."

"Don't give up just yet."

"I love your positive attitude. And on that note, I am going to drop my case file in *Post* on my desk and head home. See you in the morning."

Karen's condo was an easy walk from her office. After sitting in court all day, it felt great to stretch her legs. On the way, she passed the Happy Dragon, which had the best velvet corn and crabmeat soup in Portland. When you've spent a year in prison, where someone decides what you can and cannot do every second of the day, being able to be spontaneous is a gift from heaven. Ten minutes after she was seated, Karen celebrated her victory with a mouthful of that wonderful soup while she read a chapter of an Agatha Christie novel.

The good feeling only lasted until the maître d' seated a young man at the table next to her. He was in his twenties, dressed in a power suit. His hair and beard were professionally coiffed, and Karen guessed that he was an associate in one of the big law firms or working in finance.

Moments after he was seated, the man noticed Karen. He smiled, and she ignored him. A few moments after he ordered, he stared at her, and Karen knew what was going to happen next.

"Excuse me," the young man said. "Have we met?"

"No," Karen answered in a tone that she hoped would indicate that she did not want to continue the conversation.

"I'm sorry, but you look familiar," he said, ignoring the hint.

Karen was attractive. If she were not Karen Wyatt, she would have assumed that this was the beginning of an attempt to pick her up. But she was a celebrity, and her tale of being framed by the police, miraculously freed from prison, and awarded millions in a lawsuit had been fodder for social media and television news for months. The furor had died down, but her notoriety still enveloped her like a shroud.

Karen was certain that the man would figure out why she looked familiar very soon, and her magic moment ended, so she finished her dinner and left a twenty-dollar bill on her table before walking out of the Happy Dragon.

Karen was upset because her treasured moment had been interrupted. As soon as she got home, she changed into her pajamas and settled down with her Agatha Christie. By the time she found out whodunit, she had forgotten how upset she had been at the Happy Dragon.

CHAPTER FIVE

While Oscar Vanderlasky was dealing with Ian Mowry, Muriel Lujack returned to the Multnomah County district attorney's office. Muriel had been co-counseling the *Post* case because she had just been promoted to the unit that prosecuted felonies. Vanderlasky was supposed to be mentoring her, but very little mentoring had gone on. Vanderlasky's answers to her questions were terse and not that useful, and he resented any suggestions she made, especially when she'd pointed out the problem with the lamp.

Muriel was reading a file in a case she was going to try on her own when Vanderlasky stormed into her cubicle.

"Why did you run away when that idiot got on me?" he demanded.

"I thought you could handle him without my help."

"Well, I definitely didn't get much help from you during that fiasco."

Anyone who had been berated by nuns for twelve years was difficult to intimidate. "I told you that you should've dismissed the case as soon as I read the police reports and talked to the cops who were at the scene. They thought you were going after the wrong person."

"Yeah, well, I disagree. Post was guilty, but that bitch Wyatt twisted everything around."

"She didn't have to. I told you about the unplugged lamp. And why do you have it in for Karen Wyatt after what she went through?"

"She got what she deserved for undermining this office and the police force."

"You're kidding, right? She was framed, spent a year in prison, and lost her license to practice law. No one deserves that."

Vanderlasky realized that he didn't have a good comeback to Lujack's point, so he switched gears. "This isn't about Wyatt. This is about you not supporting me at the trial and bugging out when that asshole Mowry started in on me. I decided to prosecute Post. That's all you needed to know. I needed to know that you had my back."

Vanderlasky turned on his heels and walked away. Muriel decided that Ian Mowry hadn't been the only asshole in the courtroom that day.

An hour after Vanderlasky stomped out of her office, Muriel was summoned to the office of Ellen Kaufman, the chief criminal deputy. Kaufman was a shade over six feet with long, black hair and a muscular build. Kaufman had never married, and she lived alone on a sailboat that she took out any chance she got.

Her skin was tanned and weathered by the sun that beat down on her when she was on the water.

Kaufman had been raised by a single parent in a crime-ridden neighborhood. After working her way through college, she'd joined the police force and had been on a SWAT team when she graduated from law school, which she had attended at night.

"Shut the door and take a seat," Kaufman said when Muriel entered her office.

Kaufman's summons had made Muriel nervous, and the chief criminal deputy's serious tone did nothing to ease her tension.

"I just finished a postmortem on the *Post* case with Oscar," Kaufman said. "He had some uncomplimentary things to say about you."

The piercing blue eyes she aimed at Muriel were intimidating, but Muriel met Kaufman's stare and did not flinch.

"Did he have an explanation for the not guilty verdict?" Muriel asked.

"He did."

"I bet he didn't talk about the lamp."

Kaufman looked confused. "What lamp?"

"The one I tried to tell him would kill our case. Do you know the facts in *Post*?"

"Why don't you tell them to me."

Muriel told Kaufman about the photographs of Laurie Post that showed her injuries and the importance of the lamp. She also mentioned that the arresting officers thought that they might have arrested the wrong person.

"Thank you for filling me in," Kaufman said when Muriel finished. "You've given me a lot to think about."

"Am I in trouble?" Muriel asked.

"Absolutely not. By the way, every other person I've talked to has given you high marks. You have your first solo felony prosecution tomorrow, don't you?"

"Yes."

"Then I think you should be prepping. Good luck."

Muriel waited until she shut the door to Kaufman's office before taking a deep breath.

CHAPTER SIX

Walter Zegda was movie star handsome with the chiseled physique of a male model. In high school, he'd been the quarterback of a football team that had made the semifinals of the state championship, and he had finished third place in State as a heavyweight wrestler. Zegda's genius IQ had earned him a membership in Mensa and a perfect 4.0 GPA, which should have resulted in being valedictorian of his high school class. On paper, Zegda was the young man every parent wished their daughter would marry. Unfortunately, Zegda had one tiny flaw; he was a sadistic sociopath.

Walter had been disqualified from becoming the class valedictorian because he had been on probation. The older brother of one of Walter's friends was a member of the Lucifer's Disciples outlaw motorcycle gang. To impress him, Walter had been stealing cars that he brought to the chop shop where he was currently torturing Rob Guthrie. When he was caught, he didn't rat out the Disciples. This had impressed them. Instead of going to college or enlisting in the army, Walter had been welcomed into the club. Over the years, he had risen to a leadership position by using his brain to develop ways to make a lot of money and by using his penchant for violence to dissuade anyone who thought of challenging him.

Eventually, Zegda became second-in-command of the club. The only person standing in the way of his quest to become the gang's leader was Bull Vasquez, the club's apex predator. Then Bull disappeared. Walter opined that Vasquez had grown weary of the responsibilities of leadership and had retired to a tropical island, where he made love all day to beautiful women when he wasn't lazing on the beach drinking piña coladas. Some of the gang members thought that there might be a darker explanation for Bull's vanishing act because Bull's Harley and all his worldly possessions were still at his pad. However, these individuals kept their thoughts to themselves for fear that they too might be shipped off to the same tropical paradise where Zegda believed Bull to be residing.

Walter slapped Rob Guthrie across his face, and the lids that covered Guthrie's swollen eyes parted. He was in the garage that the Disciples used as a chop shop. Most of the garage was dark, and Rob could barely make out the cars that were lined up near the front. He could see Walter and Dennis "Wolf" Larson, because the area at the back of the garage was illuminated, but he couldn't see them too well because there was blood in his eyes.

"Hey, Rob, focus," Zegda said. "You may be a witness to history being made."

Rob tried to focus, but it was difficult, because he was strung up to the ceiling. The chain that was wrapped around his wrists had pulled him up so high that his body weight had caused his shoulders to dislocate. Rob barely felt that pain because he had been beaten senseless over the past hour, a fate Zegda felt Rob deserved for skimming profits from the drugs he was dealing for the club.

"Wolf, are you ready?" Zegda asked the massive, heavily bearded Disciple who stood next to him.

"I am," Wolf replied.

Zegda showed Rob the object he held in his hand.

"This is a Rubik's Cube, Rob. It has many colored squares. To win, you have to make each side the same color by rotating the sections of the cube. Do you follow me?"

Rob stared at Zegda. His eyes were glazed over, and drool covered his bloodstained split lips.

"Golly, Rob. You should show more interest, because your fate will be determined by how successful I am in breaking the world record for solving the cube, which now stands at three point one three seconds. I've been getting pretty close, and this will be your lucky day if I succeed. I'll be in such a good mood, I'll let you go. So, you should be rooting for me, amigo."

Zegda looked at Wolf, who was holding a stopwatch.

"Ready, set, go!" Wolf shouted.

Walter sprang into action, his fingers manipulating the cube at an amazing rate.

"Stop!" Zegda shouted as the colors on all of the sides aligned. He looked at Wolf expectantly.

Wolf shook his head. "Three point two zero, boss."

"Motherfucker," Zegda said. Then he looked at his prisoner. "Sorry, Rob. I really tried."

Zegda handed the cube to Wolf, took out a pistol, and shot Rob between his bloodshot eyes.

"Take out the trash, Wolf, while I drown my sorrows in a glass of cold beer," Zegda said, handing Wolf the gun so he could dispose of it with the body.

CHAPTER SEVEN

Silver Falls State Park, Oregon's largest state park, can be found in the middle of lush farmland about fifty miles from Portland and thirteen miles from Silverton, a city of ten thousand souls situated on the forty-fifth parallel near Salem, the state capital. The park's main attraction is the Canyon Trail, which runs through a notch in the land past ten waterfalls.

Joe and Marian Keller had spent the day picnicking in the park and wandering along the Canyon Trail. A little before dusk, they were driving back to their home in Silverton along a stretch of road bordered by farmland, when a man staggered out of a field and into the road.

"Watch out!" Marian screamed.

Joe swerved around the man and almost tipped into a ditch.

He looked in his rearview mirror and saw that the man had collapsed to one knee on the shoulder.

"Stop the car!" Marian shouted.

Joe skidded to a stop. Then he put the car in reverse and drove backward. When they were a few feet from the man, Joe parked, and the couple got out. The man was lying on his side. He was wearing a white shirt, but it was torn in places and covered in dirt. His pants were ripped at the knee, and there were bruises on his face.

Marian knelt next to the man. "Are you okay?" she asked.

The man stared at her. Joe had brought a bottle of water from the car. He handed it to the man, who took it in a shaking hand and brought it to his lips.

"What happened to you?" Marian asked.

Instead of answering the question, the man said, "I'm Tom Horan, a United States congressman, and I've been kidnapped."

Joe Keller worked in a bank, and Marian Keller taught first grade. They lived in a nice house, had plenty of friends, and were happily married, and they would have been hard-pressed to come up with anything that had happened to them that was as exciting as rescuing a kidnapped congressman. So, they could be forgiven if the first thing they did after taking Thomas Horan to the hospital was to post about their fantastic experience on Facebook and every other social media platform they could think of.

Since Salem was a hop, skip, and jump from Silverton, the *Statesman Journal* had a reporter on the Kellers' doorstep twenty minutes after someone on the paper read their first post. The newspaper scooped *The New York Times*, *The Washington Post*, CNN, Fox News, and every other news outlet in America.

As soon as Francine Horan was notified that her husband was in the hospital, she called Audrey Packer and Chad Remington.

"This should be interesting," Audrey said as they pulled into the parking lot of the hospital.

"I've been trying to figure out an explanation," Chad said. "Horan gets a call and disappears. Then his car shows up near Silverton and he wanders out of a farmer's field. Francine said that Silverton isn't in the congressman's district, and they don't know anyone who lives there."

"Silverton is near the state capital," Audrey said.

"And?"

Audrey shrugged. "That's where you find politicians."

The detectives got out of the car and walked toward the entrance to the hospital. Vans with the logos of several television stations were parked in front of the hospital, and reporters and cameramen were milling around outside. The detectives pushed their way through the crowd. One of the reporters recognized them.

"Are you here to see the congressman?" she shouted.

Packer and Remington ignored the question and walked into the lobby.

When the detectives walked out of the elevator, Francine was standing outside Horan's room talking to the doctor who was in charge of her husband's case.

"How is he doing?" Remington asked the doctor after the introductions had been made.

"Mr. Horan was dehydrated. He told me that he hadn't eaten anything for several days. He had bruises and cuts, but the cuts were superficial. His only serious injury was a blow to the head that may have left him concussed."

"Any idea what caused that wound?" Chad asked.

"I asked him, but he says that he doesn't remember. I'd guess some kind of blunt instrument."

"So, he'll be okay?" Packer asked.

"Physically, he should be fine." The doctor turned to Francine. "You may want to talk to your husband about seeing a therapist. He's depressed and shaken up from whatever it was he went through."

"Didn't he say?" Packer asked.

"He refuses to talk about it," Francine answered.

"Can we speak to Mr. Horan?" Remington asked the doctor.

"I don't see why not."

Remington turned to Francine. "We'd like to talk to him alone, if you don't mind."

"No, that's fine. Go ahead."

The detectives entered Horan's room and introduced themselves.

"How are you feeling, Congressman?" Remington asked after he and Audrey were seated next to Horan's hospital bed.

"Much better."

"So, Congressman," Audrey asked, getting right to the point, "who kidnapped you?"

"I'd rather not say."

Remington frowned. "Does that mean that you know who kidnapped you, but you don't want to tell us?"

Horan broke eye contact and looked down.

"If you know who did this . . ." Remington said.

Horan looked desperate. "If I tell you what happened, can you keep it confidential?"

"I'm really confused," Packer said. "You've been kidnapped, assaulted, and starved. Why wouldn't you want the people who did this arrested?"

"You wouldn't be able to arrest them."

"Your wife said that you got a call before you left the house. Did the person who called have anything to do with what happened?" Remington asked.

"No. Not a thing. It . . . it was something else."

"Tell us who did this, and we'll get them," Packer said. "We can bring in the FBI if necessary."

"The FBI won't be able to help."

"They're experts at dealing with kidnappings."

Horan looked desperate. "If I tell you what happened, you have to promise me that you'll keep what I tell you confidential."

Audrey and Chad looked at each other. Then Audrey nodded.

"Okay, we'll keep what you tell us between us, unless you give us permission to act on the information," Chad said. "So . . . ?"

"You'll think I'm insane."

"We're not into judging," Audrey said.

"Do you know about the UFO hearings?" Horan asked.

"I read an account," Packer said. "I didn't watch them."

"Then you know that I'm one of the biggest skeptics on the committee?"

Packer nodded.

Horan licked his lips. Then he took a deep breath. "It was aliens."

"You mean, like immigrants?" Packer said.

Remington looked confused. "What was aliens?"

"Visitors from another planet. That's who kidnapped me."

Packer's mouth opened, and she and Remington stared at Horan.

"I knew this would happen," Horan said. "That's why you can't say a word. I have an election coming up. If word of this came out, I'd be crucified."

"It would certainly cause a stir," Remington agreed.

Horan looked at him. He was angry. "Don't patronize me. Do you think this is easy for me?"

"I didn't mean to show any disrespect, but you can see that what you're saying is difficult to accept."

Horan breathed out. "I'm sorry. I shouldn't have gotten angry, but I've been through hell, and I knew how you'd react."

"Why don't you tell us what happened, so we can decide how to help you," Packer said.

"Okay, I'll tell you everything." He took another breath. "I was exhausted from the hearing, the interviews after it, and the plane ride home. Francine—my wife—picked me up at the airport. When I got home, I remember getting a call."

"Who called you?"

"I don't remember. I don't remember a lot of what happened. I do remember driving somewhere, but I'm not sure where."

"Did you drive to Silverton?" Remington asked.

Horan looked confused. "Silverton? No. That's miles from Portland. Why did you ask about Silverton?"

"It's where your car was found and near where you were found by the Kellers."

"I . . . I don't know how my car got there or how I got into that farmer's field, but I can guess."

"Sorry I interrupted you," Remington said. "Go on."

"I do remember being alone on a road when I saw these lights in the sky. I thought it was a helicopter, because it hovered over me. That's when my car stopped dead. All the lights on the dashboard and the headlights went out. The radio stopped working.

"I was confused. I didn't know what was happening. I got out of the car and walked around to the hood. I'd only taken a few steps when this beam of light came down from the craft and enveloped me. The next thing I knew, I was rising upward. Then I blacked out. When I came to, I was lying on a table and these . . . these things were examining me. I tried to move and speak, but I couldn't.

"I was spacy during the exam as if I'd been given some drug that made me sleepy. That's why my memory of what the aliens looked like is hazy. The best I can say is that they were huge and pale. They had two legs and two arms. They probed me, took skin and blood samples, and the next thing I knew, I was lying in this farmer's field. My clothes were back on, but they were ripped and dirty from lying on soil. I staggered to my feet. I was still feeling loopy. When I got my wits about me, I walked through the field until I found the road and that nice couple found me and brought me here."

Packer stared at Horan.

"You've certainly given us something to think about," Remington said, because he couldn't think of anything else he could say that wouldn't alienate—no pun intended—Thomas Horan.

"What do you think?" Remington asked Packer when they were walking to their car.

"I think we should put out an APB on a flying saucer and get arrest warrants for one or more little green men."

"Large, pale men," Remington said.

"My bad."

"I've read several stories by people who claim to have been abducted by aliens," Remington said. "Horan probably read them too when he was preparing for the hearing. His account echoes a lot of them."

"So, you think he's lying?" Packer asked.

"Or he was using a hallucinogen and had a really bad trip. If he's telling a good old-fashioned lie, the question is, why is he lying?"

"And why did he make up a story that would hold him up to ridicule? He could have just said he was carjacked."

"There is another possibility," Remington said.

"Don't go there."

"What if it's true? What if he was abducted by aliens?"

Packer shook her head. "This isn't *The X-Files*, Chad. This is the real world, not a TV show. So, I'm calling bullshit."

Remington sighed. "You're right. What do you want to do?"

"If he continues to stick to this ridiculous story, we can't do anything. He disappeared. Then he reappeared. I'd say our job was done."

PART TWO

THE PATSY

CHAPTER EIGHT

Until two days ago, Jack Blackburn had never had a high point in his life. It wasn't for lack of trying. Jack just wasn't good at anything. He did his homework and studied for tests in school, but Jack wasn't very bright, so his best efforts resulted in Cs and Ds. He was too short for basketball and too skinny for football. His final effort to get on a sports team flamed out when the bowling team coach put an arm across his shoulders and, apologetically, told Jack that they only had room on the team for ten men and, well, he was sorry, but . . .

After high school, Jack worked at odd jobs, like pizza delivery and stock boy, but his inability to perform adequately at even these jobs usually led to his being fired. Then Jack took a shot at being a criminal and failed miserably.

Jack had a few friends from high school, and they were also

losers in the game of life. One of them talked Jack into robbing a pharmacy so they could sell the drugs they looted. This turned into one of the most incompetent robberies in history. Weeks before the heist, the occupants of the building where the ground-floor pharmacy was located began calling the police to tell them that they thought that two men were casing the place. The pharmacy's large windows faced the street, its lights remained on all night, and it had a silent alarm. Moments after Jack and his friend broke in, police cars blocked the exits. Jack tried to flee, but he was caught two steps from the door. Although the DA didn't need it for a conviction, Jack shamefacedly confessed his misdeed. The judge took into account Jack's genuine remorse and the fact that this was his only brush with the law and gave him a sentence of probation with a condition that he serve two months in the county jail. And that's where he met Billy, who loaned Jack *the car*!

Jack Blackburn loved, loved, loved the 2019 Jaguar XJR575. He'd looked it up online, and, *get this*, it was exactly the type of car that was used to ferry the prime minister of fucking England and members of the royal family to state dinners. Never in his wildest dreams did Jack Blackburn ever think he would even be inside a car like this, let alone driving it all over Portland. But here he was, and here he would stay, until he found Billy and returned it, an event he knew would happen eventually but hoped never would.

Unfortunately, this high point in Jack's life didn't last long. Driving the Jag was an out-of-body experience like being on an LSD trip or smoking really good weed, and Jack was so enraptured that it took him a while to realize that the siren he was hearing and the flashing lights he was seeing in his rearview mirror were aimed at him.

Jack parked on the shoulder. Moments later, one policeman was at the driver's window and one was looking at him through the window on the passenger's side.

"Sir, please get your license and registration. Then step out of the car and keep your hands where we can see them," ordered the officer who was staring at Jack menacingly through the driver's-side window and whose name tag identified him as Brady McDowell.

Jack took the registration out of the glove box and his license out of his wallet. Before he opened the driver's door, he noticed that the officer had his hand on the butt of his gun. The other policeman's name tag identified him as Randy Wheeler. He walked around the front of the Jag and put his hand on his weapon.

"What's the trouble, Officer McDowell?" Jack asked as soon as he was outside the car.

"Let's see your license and the registration."

Jack handed them over.

"Nice wheels," McDowell said.

Jack couldn't help smiling. "This car is amazing."

"Any idea what it costs?"

"I looked it up online. It sells new for a little more than one hundred and twenty thousand."

McDowell got Jack's name from his license.

"So, Jack . . . Do you mind if I call you Jack?"

"Not at all."

"So, Jack, how are you employed?"

"I'm between jobs right now."

"Are you a trust fund baby?"

"I wish."

"Want to tell us how you can afford the Jag?"

"Oh, it's not mine."

"We know that. Want to know how? The owner reported it stolen."

"It's not stolen," Jack said. "Billy said I could drive it."

"I've got a flash for you. This isn't Billy's car. It's Terrance Cogen's, just like it says on the registration, so how did this Billy get it?"

"Billy said he's the chauffeur for the rich guy who owns it. I guess that's Mr. Cogen."

"Has Billy got a last name?"

"Of course, but I can't remember it."

"Why didn't you just return the car to the owner?"

"Uh, I, uh, I didn't know where he lived. I've been driving around Portland trying to find Billy so I could give the car back to him."

"When you couldn't find Billy, why didn't you drive to Mr. Cogen's house? The address is clearly printed on the registration papers."

"Um, I guess I didn't think of that. But I swear I didn't steal the car."

"We believe you, Jack," McDowell said in a tone dripping with sarcasm, "and we're going to help you out by going to Mr. Cogen's house. I'm sure *Billy* will clear this up."

"Great!" Jack said as he started to get back in the Jag.

"Sorry, Jack. My partner is going to drive the Jag, and you're going to ride in the back seat of our car."

Jack knew that the back seat of a police car was where prisoners rode, but he wasn't worried, because he knew that Billy would tell the officers that he had loaned Jack the car and everything would end up just fine.

They arrived at Terrance Cogen's estate a little after sunset. It was located behind a stone wall and up a winding drive in Dunthorpe, one of Portland's priciest neighborhoods. Officer McDowell drove up to the wall and was surprised to see that the wrought iron gate that was supposed to block the driveway was wide open.

When McDowell reached the end of the drive, he didn't see any lights on in the three-story mansion. McDowell parked the police car in front of a portico that covered the front entrance. His partner parked the Jag behind him.

"Does something seem off?" McDowell asked Wheeler when they were both out of their cars.

"You mean, no people."

"Yeah. A place this big, you'd think there would be someone around and lights on in the house. And why was the gate open?"

"Did you call Cogen while we were on the way?"

"Yeah. I told headquarters that we had the Jag and I got the number, but the call went to voicemail."

McDowell grew even more suspicious when he rang the doorbell and no one answered.

"Cogen's got to have help with a place this big, so where are they?" he asked as he rang the doorbell again. When there was no answer, he tried the handle. The door opened.

It was very dark in the house, and McDowell couldn't hear any sound. But he did smell a foul odor. McDowell unholstered his gun, felt along the wall, and flipped on a switch. Light from a crystal chandelier flooded the entryway, and the officers found themselves face-to-face with a snarling African lion, its claws extended and its jaws agape, displaying razor-sharp teeth.

The officers screamed and leaped back. Only their training prevented them from emptying their weapons into the taxidermied beast.

"Jesus Christ!" McDowell managed when he caught his breath. His partner was leaning forward, his hands on his knees.

McDowell looked around the massive entryway and down the halls that led off of it. Stuffed animal heads could be seen in all directions.

"Motherfucker," McDowell's partner cursed.

The officers regained their composure.

"I'm never going to the zoo again," McDowell said.

"Amen," Wheeler agreed. Then he yelled, "Police! Anyone home?"

When no one answered, the officers walked down a hall where the foul odor was strongest and into the first room on their right. McDowell felt for a light switch, flipped it on, and found himself in a massive living room. Crossed African spears hung on one wall. Frightening masks from countries around the globe were arrayed on some of the other walls above cabinets filled with artifacts of Haitian voodoo and African juju. Alongside the masks, and completely out of place, was a seascape by Turner and a Cézanne, and mixed with the African religious artifacts were a Giacometti sculpture, a marble replica of Rodin's *The Kiss*, a modern marble sculpture that resembled a Henry Moore, and several other stone and ceramic sculptures. But the main attractions in the room were a monstrous polar bear that stood on its hind legs, claws raised, and the corpse that sprawled at its feet in a pool of blood.

"Whoa," McDowell managed.

The dead man was grossly overweight and lay on his stomach. His head was turned so that McDowell couldn't see his features, but he could see the back of his head, which was covered with dried blood. Lying next to the corpse was a marble statue covered in blood and the victim's brains.

McDowell knew that there was a 99 percent possibility that the man was dead, but he checked for a pulse anyway. Then he backed out of the room.

"Let's get out of here so we don't contaminate the scene," McDowell said.

When they were outside, McDowell leaned into his car.

"What's happening?" Jack asked.

McDowell didn't answer him. He got on the car radio and told the dispatcher to get the medical examiner and homicide detectives to the house. When he ended his call, he walked toward the Jaguar. His partner met him halfway. He was carrying a wallet in a plastic evidence bag.

"I found this in the glove compartment buried under some stuff. It's empty, except for one credit card belonging to Terrance Cogen. It also has a stain that looks like blood."

McDowell walked back to the police car and got in the front seat so he was facing Jack Blackburn.

"Mr. Blackburn, I am placing you under arrest for the murder of Terrance Cogen."

CHAPTER NINE

Audrey Packer and Chad Remington were next up on the homicide rotation, so they caught the Terrance Cogen homicide.

"Have you ever been inside one of these mansions?" Audrey asked her partner as they turned off the highway and into Dunthorpe.

"About ten years ago. A financial analyst committed suicide when his company went under and his wife walked out."

"I've never been. Was it nice?"

"The house?"

"Yeah."

"It was too big. I would have rattled around in it."

"You could have held parties to fill it up. Was there a pool?"

"Yeah. We found the poor bastard floating in it."

They turned a corner and saw the police car sitting beside the

FALSE WITNESS

open gate. Packer held her ID out of the driver's-side window, and the uniform waved them through. An ambulance and several cars, marked and unmarked, were parked in a turnaround. The most conspicuous vehicle was a Jaguar that Chad guessed cost more than he made in a year.

Packer parked, and the detectives got out of their car.

Brady McDowell knew Packer and Remington from cases they had worked, and he walked over.

"Hey," McDowell said.

"I understand you caught the perp," Audrey said.

McDowell pointed his thumb over his shoulder. "He's in the back of my car. He hasn't asked for a lawyer, so you want to take a shot?"

"Sounds good," Chad said. "Fill us in."

McDowell told the detectives about spotting the stolen Jag and finding Cogen's body. The detectives cracked up when McDowell told them about being freaked out by the lion.

"Has Blackburn admitted to killing Cogen?"

"No. He says he's never been in the house, and he insists that this Billy guy loaned him the car."

"Have you talked to Billy?"

"We didn't find anyone on the property. Someone was living in an apartment over the garage, but it looks like they cleared out."

"Okay. Take me to Mr. Blackburn," Remington said.

Jack Blackburn pressed his face against the window when McDowell and the detectives walked up. McDowell had told the detectives that he didn't think the suspect would try anything, so Chad opened the back door.

"Hi, Jack. I'm Chad Remington, a detective with Homicide, and this is my partner, Audrey Packer."

Blackburn looked sick. "Why did they send homicide detectives? I haven't killed anyone."

"I hear you've been cooped up for a while. Would you like to take a walk and get some fresh air?"

"Yeah, thank you. Does that mean I can get out of the car?"

"It does. Just don't go running off. I'm getting too old to chase you, so I'd have to shoot you."

"I won't run. I promise."

"I was just fucking with you, Jack. If you didn't kill Mr. Cogen, you wouldn't have a reason to run, would you?"

"No, sir."

Jack got out of the car, and he and Chad started strolling across the lawn that bordered the mansion. Audrey and McDowell trailed behind.

"Why did you lie to Officer McDowell about not knowing where Mr. Cogen lived?"

Jack hung his head. "I shouldn't have done that, but I was scared he'd arrest me for stealing the Jag."

"Tell me about the car."

Jack's face lit up, and he waxed poetic about his dream car.

"Why do you think Billy let you drive the Jag?" Chad asked.

"He was too drunk to drive. He asked me to take his girlfriend home."

"Does the girlfriend have a name?"

"I think it's Candy or Cindy. I'm not sure. She didn't say much at the bar after Billy introduced her, so I only heard the name once."

"Why do you think Billy didn't try to get the car back? It's pretty expensive, and it doesn't belong to him."

"I don't know. I'm not sure if I told him where I live."

"But you knew Billy worked here. Why not drive here and return the car?"

"I should have."

"You ever watch crime shows on TV, Jack?"

"Sometimes."

"You know that the guys from the crime lab are going to go over this crime scene with a fine-tooth comb. If they find a hair or a piece of skin belonging to you or a fingerprint or DNA in this house, after you've said that you've never been inside, you know you're fucked. So, I'm going to ask you if you still say you were never inside the house."

"I swear to God I never was."

"Okay, then."

Chad turned and headed back toward the house. Blackburn followed him.

"Are you gonna let me go?" Jack asked.

"Not right now."

Chad returned Blackburn to McDowell and told the officer to take his prisoner downtown and book him. Then Remington led Audrey into Cogen's mansion.

Dr. Sally Grace, the medical examiner, was just leaving. Dr. Grace was a slender woman with frizzy black hair, who had a dry sense of humor and a sharp intellect. She had testified in several of Chad's trials, and he thought she was an excellent witness.

"What's the word?" Packer asked.

"Today's word is *blunt force trauma*," Sally answered.

"That's three words," Packer said.

"One for each blow our victim received. And he was probably killed a few days ago. I'll have more for you after the autopsy."

Dr. Grace left, and the detectives walked past the lion and down the hall to the scene of the crime. Audrey stared at the polar bear.

"How many shots do you think it took to bring that thing down?"

"I have no idea," Chad answered, "and I hope I never have to find out."

The men from the medical examiner's office had waited for

the detectives to arrive before taking the body away. They stood aside when Packer and Remington walked in.

Chad didn't have a medical degree, but he thought that he could have diagnosed the cause of death as easily as the medical examiner. Someone had destroyed Terrance Cogen's skull with a heavy, blood-drenched marble statue. Brain and bone fragments lay near the corpse, and blood formed a halo around the dead man's head. Chad had been to many crime scenes, but he put this one in his top ten for sheer violence.

"Was Cogen married?" Chad asked.

"I did an internet search before we left. Rosemarie and Terrance Cogen are separated, and she lives in a penthouse near the Portland Art Museum."

"Let's visit the widow," Chad said.

Twenty minutes later, the detectives were in the lobby of the condominium where Rosemarie Cogen was living. They flashed their IDs and told the security guard that they needed to speak to Mrs. Cogen. He called up to the penthouse. Then he led the detectives past a bank of elevators in the lobby to another elevator and keyed them up to the top floor.

"You have better people skills, so why don't you break the news to Mrs. Cogen?" Packer said.

When the elevator doors opened, the detectives found themselves in a marble entryway that led to a sunken living room. A tall woman in her midthirties with blue eyes, raven-colored hair that fell to her shoulders, and an athletic figure was standing a few feet from the elevator. She had a glass in her hand and looked puzzled.

"Mrs. Cogen?" Chad asked.

"Call me Rosemarie. Milton said you are detectives."

"We are. My name is Chad Remington, and this is my

partner, Audrey Packer. I'm afraid we have some bad news for you. Can we go into the living room, where you can find a comfortable seat?"

"Certainly. Can I get you something to drink?" Rosemarie held up her glass. "I make a mean martini, but I have a full bar."

"Nothing for me," Remington said.

"I'll pass too," Packer said.

"Then join me," Cogen said as she led the way down a short flight of steps and motioned the detectives toward a long couch facing floor-to-ceiling windows that provided a stunning view of the lights of Portland.

"Now, what is so serious that you want me to sit down?"

"I'm sorry to have to tell you that your husband has passed away," Chad said.

Rosemarie's full lips formed a pleasant smile. "You mean he's dead?"

"Yes, ma'am."

The smile widened. "What's the bad news?" she asked.

Audrey frowned. "My partner forgot to tell you that we're from Homicide, and your husband has been brutally murdered in the living room of his mansion."

"*My* mansion."

"Pardon me?" Chad said.

"I own this penthouse and the estate in Dunthorpe. Terrance didn't own squat."

"You don't appear to be upset by the news of your husband's death," Audrey said.

"Sorry to disappoint you, but Terrance was a crook and an asshole, and his death means that I won't have to continue paying my divorce lawyer."

"Why do you say Mr. Cogen was a crook?" Packer asked.

Cogen shrugged. "He was being investigated by the feds and the Multnomah County DA. Since you're in law enforcement, you can probably find out the details. All I know is that we lived in this building before Terrance and I separated, and he moved back to that mausoleum in Dunthorpe. Terrance was the building treasurer. From what I've heard, there were projects that cost millions but were never started. I've been told that the money went to shell companies Terrance owned, and antique cars and artwork suddenly appeared in Dunthorpe."

"Did you know he was stealing?"

"Terrance never confided in me about where money was coming from. I thought he made it in the stock market and his business as a financial adviser, but since my lawyer started looking, I've discovered that he was a very unsuccessful trader and his clients tended to lose money."

"Can you think of a person who might have killed your husband?" Remington asked.

Rosemarie smiled. "You mean, besides me? Well, detectives, there were the people he scammed. I understand that embezzling from this building wasn't his only criminal enterprise. But, as I said, I don't know the details of his criminal activities."

"When was the last time you saw your husband?" Packer asked.

"Let me see. We met at his lawyer's office three days ago." Rosmarie grimaced. "That was fun. Terrance was foaming at the mouth and calling me names I couldn't repeat in the presence of children, which, thank God, we don't have."

"Does he have any?" Packer asked.

"Two from his first wife. Marta lives in Arizona. I think she's an accountant. Terrance Jr. lives in Manhattan, where, from what Terrance told me, he is a failed actor."

"How many times has Mr. Cogen been married?" Remington asked.

"I'm number four, and I should have known better, but, as I've discovered, Terrance was an ace number one con man."

"The person we've arrested for your husband's murder was driving one of your husband's cars." Packer consulted the notes. "A 2019 Jaguar XJR575."

Rosemarie shrugged. "I don't know anything about Terrance's cars, and I could not care less."

"The reason I ask is that the man claims that someone named Billy lent him the car and said he was your husband's chauffeur. Did your husband employ a chauffeur named Billy?"

"That would be Billy Kramer."

"Do you know where we can find him? There wasn't anyone at the house in Dunthorpe."

"Billy was living in an apartment over the garage."

"We did find the apartment, but no one was there, and it looked like whoever had been living there had cleared out," Chad said.

"Sorry, I can't help you."

"Were there other servants?"

"Cynthia Woodruff kept house and Terrance had a cook named Alvin Martelli, but they didn't live at the estate. Terrance dealt with the staff. I imagine he'd have their numbers and addresses in his phone."

"Do I take it that you lived here and your husband lived in Dunthorpe?" Chad asked.

"My grandfather made a ton of money in logging, and he built the Dunthorpe mansion to show off how well he'd done. Daddy squandered most of the fortune, and the place started to go to pot. I never liked the estate, and I got out of there as soon as I could. Terrance used the place to impress the people he was scamming. But I was going to boot him out as soon as the divorce was final."

"Was Mr. Cogen the big-game hunter?" Chad asked.

Rosemarie laughed. "I see you've met Leo the lion and Teddy the bear."

"We have," Chad said. "The lion scared the hell out of the first officers on the scene."

"Daddy bagged those sad beasts. Terrance wouldn't have been caught dead in deepest, darkest Africa. Too untidy."

The detectives spent another half hour with Mrs. Cogen before leaving.

"What did you think of the widow Cogen?" Remington asked when they were walking to their car.

"I like the fact that she didn't put on an act."

"We do have to put her on our list of suspects."

"Of course. But I hope she didn't kill Cogen," Packer said. "I like her."

CHAPTER TEN

Jack Blackburn was scared. He'd been in jail before, but that had gone okay. No one had tried to beat him up or rape him like they did in the TV shows, and his cellmate had been a nice guy. His sentence had been probation with only two months locked up. His lawyer had told him that he would probably get out sooner if he behaved himself. The lawyer had been right. So, it was in and out. Jack knew that it wouldn't go that way if he was convicted of murder.

Jack wasn't sleeping much. Jail nights were not peaceful nights. There were mentally disturbed inmates who screamed, there were inmates who sobbed, and there were inmates who threatened to kill the men who were robbing them of sleep. When he did drift off, he had terrible nightmares that left him exhausted and frightened when he woke from them.

Worst of all was not knowing what was going to happen. He didn't have the money to hire an attorney who could let him know what was going on, and he didn't know anyone who would lend him what it would take to get a good lawyer. He didn't have many friends in Portland, and there weren't any he could hit up for lawyer money, because they were as poor as he was.

Relatives weren't an answer either. He was an only child. His parents had divorced when he was young. His father was dead, and his mother lived in Utah. They didn't get along, and she was on welfare anyway.

Jack was lying on his bed in his cell worrying when the guard told him that his lawyer was waiting for him and let him out of his cell. That confused Jack, but he followed the guard so he could find out why a lawyer would be visiting him.

Prior to 1983, the Multnomah County jail was an antiquated, fortresslike edifice constructed of huge granite blocks that was located on Rocky Butte, several miles from downtown Portland. When the Rocky Butte jail was torn down to make way for the I-205 freeway, the detention center was moved to the fourth through tenth floors of the Justice Center, a sixteen-story concrete-and-glass building located across a park from the old courthouse in downtown Portland.

Karen and Morris walked through the Justice Center's vaulted lobby, past the curving stairs that led to the courtrooms on the third floor, and through a pair of glass doors that opened into the jail reception area. They showed their IDs at reception, then walked through a metal detector to an elevator that took them to the floor with the contact visiting rooms. When the elevator doors opened, the lawyer and her investigator found themselves in a narrow corridor with a thick metal door at one end. Affixed to the pastel-yellow concrete wall next to the door was an intercom. Moments after Karen used it, electronic locks snapped open, and a guard ushered them into another narrow corridor that ran in front of three contact visiting rooms. Each one had a large shatterproof window that let the guards see what was going on in each room.

The guard opened the door to the middle room. A molded plastic chair stood on each side of a table that was bolted to the floor. Karen took one of the chairs, and Morris leaned against the wall. Moments later, a second guard opened another steel door in the back wall, and Jack Blackburn shuffled into the room wearing an orange jumpsuit that seemed to swallow his skinny body.

Blackburn's unkempt, straight blond hair swept across his forehead, shading dull blue eyes. He was so pale that any color he might have had seemed to have been bleached out of his complexion.

Karen stood up. "My name is Karen Wyatt, and I've been asked by the court to represent you. This is Morris Johnson, my investigator. He'll be helping us find the evidence that can clear your name."

Blackburn flashed a weary smile. "I can't pay you, Miss Wyatt. I'm not working right now, and I'm pretty broke."

"That doesn't matter. The judge appointed me to help you out at the state's expense. You don't have to worry about being able to afford an attorney."

Blackburn looked relieved. "That's great. Thank you."

"How are you feeling? Jail must be tough," Karen said when Blackburn took the empty seat.

"I was in once before. That's how I got in this mess."

Karen had read through the discovery provided by the district attorney's office before coming to the jail, but she wanted to find out how Blackburn's version of events might differ from the police reports.

"Why don't you tell us what happened."

Blackburn flushed with embarrassment and looked down at the top of the table. "This is all my fault. I was stupid, and I listened to Preston. He said we could rob the pharmacy, that it would be easy. But it wasn't, and we got caught. The judge was fair. He gave me probation, but he said I had to go to jail for two months, and that's where I met Billy, who was in for a bar fight.

"One day, after I got out of jail, I was walking down Broadway, and I saw Billy. He was dressed real nice, so I asked him what he was doing. He told me that he was working as a chauffeur and houseman for this rich guy, and it was his day off. Then he took me to this restaurant and treated me to lunch and a beer."

"Did he say who the rich guy was?"

Blackburn looked away, and he hesitated before answering. "I don't think he told me his name. If he did, I don't remember."

"Sorry to interrupt. Go on."

"I'm pretty good with cars, and I had a job working at a garage when we had lunch. I gave Billy my phone number and said they did good work and I could get his boss a discount.

"I didn't hear from Billy for a while. Then, a few days ago, he called me and said he wanted to get together. I told him I wasn't working at the garage anymore, but he said that didn't matter. It was late, about nine, but I wasn't doing anything, so I said sure.

"Billy told me to meet him at the Clinton Street Tavern, which wasn't far from where I was staying. I didn't have a car, so I walked over. Billy was waiting in a booth way in the back, and he had this girl with him. I think he said her name was Candy or Cindy or something like that. She looked nervous and didn't say much, and Billy talked a lot. I thought he might be high, and he definitely seemed nervous.

"Anyway, after we'd had a few beers and shot the shit, his girlfriend said she wasn't feeling well and wanted to go home. Billy said he'd had one drink too many and didn't want to drive. He gave me his keys and told me his car was parked in a garage nearby and asked if I'd drive Cindy or Candy home, then come back with the car. I said sure.

"Cindy—I'll call her that—took me to the garage, and I saw the car. I couldn't believe it. I mean, I never dreamed I'd ever drive a car like that."

"This was the Jag?" Karen asked.

"Not just any Jaguar. It was an XJR575. You know what they cost?"

"I read the police report."

"They use that car to drive the king of England around! It was like I'd died and gone to heaven, because I had to think that heaven was the only place I'd ever get a shot at driving a car like that."

Blackburn shook his head. "I should have known better. Nothing ever goes my way." He flashed a sad smile. "You know that saying, 'If I didn't have bad luck, I wouldn't have any luck at all'? That's the story of my life."

"Did you drive Cindy home?" Karen asked to get Blackburn back on track.

"Yeah, or I thought I did. She had me let her off at a corner. She waited there until I drove off. I never saw her go into a house."

"Do you think Billy set you up?"

"Now I do, 'cause when I got back to the bar, he was gone. I asked the bartender if he knew where Billy went, but he didn't know who I was talking about."

"So, you kept the car?"

"Well, I had to, didn't I? I had no idea where Billy lived. And now that I had the Jag, I was worried sick. I don't live in the best neighborhood, and I was afraid someone would steal the car or do something to it. I paid for a spot in a parking garage, even though I really couldn't afford it."

"Why were you driving the car when you were arrested?"

"Honest to God, I was looking all over for Billy. Just cruising and hoping I'd see him so I could give back the Jag."

"There's a problem with what you just said. You didn't want to give the car back, did you?"

Blackburn's cheeks turned bright red. Karen looked Blackburn in the eye until he looked away.

"You don't lie very well, Jack. If you tell a jury what you just told me, do you know what the DA will ask you?"

"No."

"He'll ask you why you didn't drive to Terrance Cogen's house and return the car. If you say you didn't know he was the owner, that tricky DA will hand you the registration with Cogen's name and address on it that was in the glove box. What will you say if he does that?"

Blackburn looked at the tabletop while he thought about how he would answer the DA's question. When he realized that he wouldn't be able to bluff, he looked up.

"You got me." Blackburn sighed. "I loved that car, and I never wanted to give it back. I figured that Billy would get in touch and tell me where to bring the car and I'd get to drive it until he did."

"So, you did look at the registration?"

Blackburn nodded.

"And you knew where Cogen lived."

"Yeah, but I never went there, and I didn't know that Cogen had been murdered."

"When you opened the glove box, did you see the wallet?"

"I saw it, but I'm not a thief. I never used the credit card."

"Did you notice the bloodstain?"

"Honest, I didn't know it was blood. I looked through the wallet. Then I put it back. That's all."

"Which explains how your prints got on it."

"I guess."

"There's one more problem, Jack. The police found a beer glass on a table near Cogen's body. It had your fingerprints on it."

"What?!"

"How did that get there?"

Suddenly, Blackburn looked angry. "He *did* set me up! I drank a glass of beer at the bar. Billy must have taken the glass and put it in Cogen's house."

"If that's true, he probably killed his boss and framed you," Karen said.

Blackburn looked grim. "That sounds about right."

"What do you think?" Karen asked Morris Johnson when they were on the street walking back to the office.

"I'm skeptical," her investigator answered. "Every felon who was ever arrested with stolen goods didn't know the goods were stolen and met some guy in a bar who sold it to them cheap."

"But we know Billy exists. Mrs. Cogen told the detectives a Billy Kramer was her husband's houseman and chauffeur. And Cindy could be Cynthia Woodruff."

"True. Where do you think they are?"

"Long gone, if they murdered Terrance Cogen."

"Blackburn could have done it. He was convicted for burglary. He goes to Dunthorpe and cases Cogen's place, breaks in, kills Cogen, and steals the car."

"And has a glass of beer with his victim before bumping him off?"

"That's a good point."

"Go to the Clinton Street Tavern and see what you can find out. Then head over to Cynthia Woodruff's apartment. The address is in the police reports."

CHAPTER ELEVEN

The address for Cynthia Woodruff listed in the police report was for an old brick building in Northwest Portland. Johnson called his wife and said he might be late. Then he parked near the building and walked up three flights to Woodruff's apartment.

When the investigator knocked on Woodruff's door and got no response, he walked down to the first floor where the landlord lived.

"Mr. Fong?" Morris asked the man who opened the door.

"Yes?"

"I just came from Cynthia Woodruff's apartment. I need to talk to her, but she's not in. I was wondering if you might know where she is."

The landlord eyed Johnson suspiciously. "Why do you want to talk to her?"

Morris handed the landlord his card. "Sorry, I should have explained. Miss Woodruff worked for a man named Terrance Cogen. He was murdered recently. I'm an investigator. My boss is representing the person who was arrested for the crime. He says that he's innocent, and we think Miss Woodruff may be able to prove he is. That's why I have to talk to her."

"Good luck with that. Woodruff took off without paying her rent. If you find her, let me know."

"That's too bad, and I'll definitely get in touch if we find her." Morris paused. Then he pretended to get an idea. "Say, do you think you could let me into her place? She may have left something behind that will help me find her."

Mr. Fong hesitated. Then he shrugged.

"Normally, I wouldn't, but I don't owe her anything, since she stiffed me. Wait a minute while I get the key."

A few minutes later, Morris was standing in the dark entryway of a one-bedroom apartment. Hot air had been trapped in the confined space, and Morris detected the faint smell of cooked meat.

A couch stood against the wall that had a door that led into a tiny bedroom. Women's magazines with suggestions for meeting men and enhancing a woman's sex life were strewn across a coffee table. A television was attached to the wall beside a window across from the couch and coffee table. The window looked out on a park, the only thing that brightened the dismal space.

A sink, stove, and small refrigerator stood against another wall. Lying in an unwashed frying pan on the stove were the remnants of a hamburger. A plate with a half-eaten burger and a glass half-filled with beer sat on a place mat on a yellow Formica-topped table. Woodruff had left without finishing her meal. Had a frenzied call from Billy Kramer made her flee?

In the bedroom, Morris saw more indications of a hasty exit. The door to the room's only closet was wide open. There were no clothes on the hangers, and several hangers were spread across the floor.

The drawers in a chest of drawers were half open. Morris looked in them and found a single sock pressed against the back of one of the drawers, the only indication that it once held Cynthia's clothing.

Morris spent a few more minutes searching the apartment. Mr. Fong was waiting for Morris in the hall outside the apartment.

"Did you find where she's gone?" he asked.

Morris shook his head. "Did Miss Woodruff own a car?"

"Yeah, but it's not here. I looked."

"What can you tell me about her?"

"Not much. She kept to herself. Until now, she paid her rent on time. I know she had a job as a maid for some rich man. She told me his name once, but I don't remember it. She wasn't around much during the week. I guess she was at work.

"She did have a boyfriend. He came here on occasion. I'm sure he spent the night every once in a while, but I didn't see him here much."

"What did the boyfriend look like?"

"He was a big guy, good-looking, well-built. I think he had blond hair." Fong shrugged. "I don't remember anything more about him."

"Okay. Thanks. You've been a big help. If Miss Woodruff gets in touch or if you think of anything else, will you give me a call?"

Fong said he would, and Morris walked to his car. Jack Blackburn had described Billy Kramer, and Morris was certain that Kramer was the boyfriend. The big question was whether Kramer and Woodruff had fled because they were guilty of murder or for some other reason.

CHAPTER TWELVE

Wolf Larson, second-in-command of the Lucifer's Disciples, scanned the Happy Bean Coffee Shop until he found Walter Zegda, wearing the Disciples colors, sitting in the back at a table surrounded by a circle of unpopulated tables. Zegda liked to meet in random coffee shops to discuss serious gang business for three reasons. First, Zegda was paranoid, and he was certain that federal and state police forces had placed bugs in every tavern where the Disciples congregated. Second, the type of people who patronized coffee shops would not want to sit anywhere near massive, ferocious, motorcycle gang members decked out in gang colors, thus ensuring that his conversations would not be overheard. Third, Zegda was addicted to soy caramel lattes. He even had an espresso machine and caramel syrup in the Disciples' clubhouse.

Zegda was sipping his favorite drink and reading Victor Hugo's *Les Misérables* in the original French when Wolf sat down.

"Billy is in the wind, and so is his girlfriend," Wolf said.

"Hmm," Zegda answered as he put a bookmark between the pages of his book and closed it. "Witness protection?"

"Nah. I just think he skipped."

"Well, that's a problem, isn't it? Mr. Kramer has a lot of information he could use against us if he's arrested."

"That's a scary thought. What do you want to do?"

"Get the word out to our affiliates and anyone else you can think of to bring him in. Offer a reward. Billy isn't very bright, so our efforts should be rewarded rather quickly."

"What about the girl?" Wolf asked.

"I really don't care. Anything that happens..." Zegda shrugged. "She's collateral damage."

Zegda grabbed his book and his latte and left with Wolf right behind him. When the door closed behind the duo, the tension level in the coffee shop dropped to zero.

PART THREE

THE TRAITOR

CHAPTER THIRTEEN

A few months earlier, Raymond Castor and several other members of the Lucifer's Disciples got into a fight with a group of construction workers in a tavern near the gang's clubhouse. Raymond, whose nickname was Ray-Ray, had smashed a beer glass against the skull of one of the construction workers, sending him to the hospital with a concussion and numerous cuts and bruises. The last time Mr. Castor had been in a bar fight, his right cheek had been sliced open from just below his eye to his jawline, and the construction worker had made a positive identification as soon as he saw the vivid scar on Castor's face in his mug shot.

Muriel Lujack had been assigned to prosecute Castor. She had finished an interview with the victim an hour ago, and she was making notes for his direct examination when the receptionist told her that a Miss Nikki Randolph was in the waiting room and wanted to see her. Muriel was about to tell the receptionist that she was busy when she remembered seeing Randolph listed as Ray-Ray's girlfriend in a police report.

There were several people in the waiting area, but there was no question which one was Nikki Randolph. The helmet she held in her lap, her black leather jacket, heavy jeans, and black T-shirt gave her away. Muriel guessed that Nikki was six feet tall and weighed close to two hundred pounds, which made her an ideal mate for Ray-Ray, who was six-five and weighed two ninety.

"Hi, Miss Randolph. I'm Muriel Lujack, and I'm handling Ray-Ray's case. I understand you want to see me."

"Yeah, I do." Randolph looked around reception. She seemed uncomfortable. "Is there somewhere more private we could talk?"

"Sure. Let's see if one of the conference rooms is available."

Moments later, Muriel was seated across from Ray-Ray's girlfriend on one side of a long conference table. Nikki looked very nervous, and Muriel smiled in an attempt to put her at ease.

"Why do you want to see me?" Lujack asked.

"I know Ray-Ray hurt that guy, but they were fighting. I don't know why you aren't going after the other guy."

"You weren't in the bar, were you?"

"No."

"We decided to charge Ray-Ray because Mr. Shaw didn't use a weapon and Ray-Ray hit him with a beer glass and caused some serious injuries."

"Ray-Ray told me he was just defending himself."

"I'm sure his lawyer will argue that to the jury."

"Is there any way you could just dismiss the case?"

"Not without a good reason now that the grand jury handed down an indictment."

Randolph hunched her shoulders and took a deep breath. "What if I could tell you something important about a big case?"

"What sort of case?"

"The murder of a cop. If it helped you find who killed him, could you cut Ray-Ray some slack?"

"Is this something Ray-Ray knows?"

"Yeah."

"Would he tell me what he knows?" Muriel asked, even though she knew that no Lucifer's Disciple would ever make a deal with a DA.

"No. I shouldn't even be here. But with his past record, Ray-Ray could go to prison for years, and I can't live without him."

"Why don't we do this?" Muriel said. "You tell me what you know, and I'll promise not to tell anyone what you tell me or that it was you who told me, even if it's very important, unless you agree that I can use the information. I'll pretend that you were never here. If what you tell me is useful in bringing a cop killer to justice, I'll help Ray-Ray."

The conference room had a view, but Randolph stared at the river and the mountains without seeing them. It was obvious that Randolph was torn between helping her boyfriend and violating the Disciples' code.

"If this gets back to Ray-Ray or any of the Disciples, I'll be in for a world of hurt."

"I understand."

"Okay." Randolph took a deep breath. "You know that lawyer, Karen Wyatt, who was framed?"

Muriel felt like she'd been hit with a Taser. She nodded.

"The reason she was framed was because the Disciples had a cop and a DA on their payroll, and they arranged for the cops to raid the Demon Slayers' clubhouse so they could get their drug business. Wyatt showed that this was a setup and that a cop and a DA were involved. But they weren't the only ones in with the Disciples. A cop named Max Ellis was on the payroll, and so was one more crooked DA.

"When that lab guy told about the frame, they had to get rid of Ellis, because the lab guy could ID Ellis and Ellis could ID the DA. So he was snuffed. What Ray-Ray told me was that the crooked DA was high up."

"Did Ray-Ray give you a name?"

"No. It was just something he said one night when we were talking after Ellis was killed. He said he knew who it was, but he never told me."

Muriel felt like her brain was on fire, and she took a moment to compose herself. "How do you know I'm not the DA who's on the take?"

Randolph smiled. "I did some research. You were still in law school when Wyatt was framed, and I talked to a few people. I know they call you 'the Nun' because you're such a straight arrow."

The nickname didn't upset Lujack. She liked it. It was not embarrassing to be known as someone who was ethical and honest.

"Nikki, you've given me a lot to think about. I want you safe, so don't contact me. You'll know I used what you gave me if I make a deal that helps Ray-Ray."

Muriel escorted Nikki Randolph to the waiting room. Then she returned to her cubicle and tried to work on Castor's case, but she kept drifting, distracted by the fact that someone she worked with was responsible for the murder of Max Ellis and sending Karen Wyatt to prison.

Who was the traitor? Frank Curtin had just been elected to the post of Multnomah district attorney and had not been in the office when Karen Wyatt was framed. But he had run on a platform that involved decriminalizing drugs, which would have benefited the Disciples.

Muriel made a list of people who had been working in the office four years earlier. Oscar Vanderlasky came to mind immediately. He hated Wyatt and had prosecuted the case that sent

Wyatt to prison. Ellen Kaufman had been in the office forever. Janet Kim was in charge of the lawyers who prosecuted narcotics cases, and drugs were heavily involved in the crimes that had led to Wyatt's incarceration. And there were other deputy district attorneys who had been in the office when Wyatt was framed. How could she figure out the identity of the traitor? After giving the question a lot of thought, Muriel decided that she would have to learn as much as she could about the raid on the Demon Slayers motorcycle club, so she went to the room where the files of closed cases were kept and asked the clerk for the files in the case of *State of Oregon v. William Harold Baer*.

Muriel headed home around six. She lived in a small apartment. The living room was outfitted with a sofa, a coffee table, a small television set, and a bookshelf crammed full of books that stood next to an armchair on which a standing lamp cast its glow.

Muriel brought the remnants of a salad she found in the back of her refrigerator to her dining room table and picked at it while she read through the files in the *Baer* case.

What Muriel read was disturbing. Karen Wyatt had represented William Baer, who was accused of assaulting one of the policemen who raided the Demon Slayers' clubhouse. Ellen Kaufman had represented the State because of the notoriety the case had generated. Baer was second-in-command of the Demon Slayers and the person with connections to a Mexican cartel that was supplying the gang with the heroin they were selling. The Lucifer's Disciples were in competition with the Slayers and wanted Baer out of the way so they could cripple the club's connection to the cartel.

During the raid, Baer was beaten severely by Officer Chet Stevens, who claimed that Baer had attacked him. Baer said that he'd surrendered as soon as the police stormed in. Stevens didn't know that Wayne Costner, the leader of the Slayers, suspected one of the members of stealing heroin to feed an addiction and had secretly installed security cameras just before the raid. After Stevens testified on direct, Karen had destroyed him by showing footage of Stevens beating her client after it was clear that he had given up. The cameras also caught two other police officers stealing money and drugs from the Slayers.

After Baer was acquitted, Stevens and the other officers had been arrested. A special prosecutor from the state attorney general's office had been appointed to handle the case, and Stevens had made a deal for a lighter sentence. As part of the deal, he'd said that Donna Ridley, a deputy district attorney, had been paid by the Disciples to work up a search warrant for the Demon Slayers' clubhouse. To support the request for the warrant, Stevens provided the testimony of an anonymous informant, who did not exist, and Ridley wrote the search warrant affidavit.

Stevens and Ridley had been bribed and told what to do by Robert Barbour, a low-ranking member of the Disciples. Barbour's body was found in a roadside ditch soon after Baer's trial, and Stevens and Ridley said that they did not meet with any other gang member, so the trail to the Disciples had gone cold.

The investigators had asked many questions about Walter Zegda, who was easily the most interesting person mentioned in the file. Stevens and Ridley knew that giving the authorities Zegda would be rewarded with a golden ticket, but it would also be a death sentence. Neither one implicated Zegda in the plot.

Muriel didn't think she was any closer to figuring out the identity of the traitor in the DA's office after reading the file, and she had no idea how to discover the traitor's identity. Muriel knew that a few investigative reporters had tried to solve that mystery, but as far as she knew, nothing had ever come of their efforts. Now, Muriel had new information.

She was too tired to think clearly, so she closed her laptop, turned on her television, and found a channel that streamed classic movies. *Casablanca* was playing. It was one of her favorite movies, and she couldn't remember how many times she'd seen it. When it was over, she climbed into bed. As soon as she closed her eyes, the question that had troubled her all evening reared its head. Should she tell Karen Wyatt what she had learned from Nikki Randolph? By the time she fell asleep, she still didn't know the answer.

CHAPTER FOURTEEN

"What is so important that you interfered with my lunch?" Chad Remington asked Audrey Packer when she stopped her unmarked car in front of the food cart where Remington had been eating.

"We are returning to the scene of the crime."

"Which crime scene?"

"The Dunthorpe estate."

"And why are we doing that?"

"To get you ice cream for dessert to make up for interfering with your lunch."

"Sounds good. Want to tell me why you're being so good to me?"

"The medical examiner found ice cream laced with sedatives in Cogen's stomach, and I want to check out something."

"Okay."

"And I have another surprise for you. Want to guess whose fingerprints were found in Cogen's house?"

"Do I get to ask twenty questions?"

"You do not."

"Can you give me a hint?"

"The person works in Washington, DC, and recently took a ride in a flying saucer."

"You're shitting me."

"I am not."

Remington had only been inside the kitchen in the Dunthorpe house briefly on his first visit to the crime scene. He thought it was only a little bit smaller than his condo. There were two sinks. One was filled with dirty dishes. Cabinets lined up above the two sinks, a stove with several burners, a large microwave, and two dishwashers. A granite-topped island stretched across the room under a long rack from which various types of shiny pots and pans dangled. The island divided the stove and other utilities from a large refrigerator and a separate freezer.

"What are we looking for?" Remington asked as he followed Audrey into the kitchen. His partner walked to the freezer without answering and opened it. When she saw the many tubs of ice cream, she smiled.

"I was lying about dessert. If you eat any of this ice cream, I'll have to arrest you for tampering with evidence."

"Gee, thanks."

"Now let's find the blender."

It took several minutes searching the cabinets to find a blender. Audrey set it on the island.

"Did you see the dirty dishes in the sink?"

"Yeah."

"There isn't a glass with traces of ice cream, and this blender has been washed. What do you deduce from these facts, Watson?"

"Cogen was really fat. From all of the ice cream in the freezer, I deduce that he drank a lot of milkshakes. Our killer put sedatives in a milkshake, bashed in Cogen's head when he passed out, and washed the glass and blender to disguise the fact that Cogen had been drugged."

"Very good. You have the makings of an excellent sidekick."

Chad smiled. Then he got serious. "Now what?"

"Now, we have a heart-to-heart with Congressman Horan."

"He's in the den," Francine Horan said. "He's been holed up in there since he got out of the hospital."

"How is he doing?" Remington asked.

"Honestly, he . . ." Francine looked frustrated. "I can't get him to go out. He seems scared to death, and he's having horrible nightmares. He wakes up in a sweat, screaming. It's really scaring me."

"Why don't we talk to him. It might help clear up some of the things that are frightening him," Remington said.

Francine led the way to the den, then closed the door and left the detectives with her husband. Horan looked startled when the detectives walked in. He hadn't shaved in days, and he was wearing pajamas.

"Why are you here?" Horan demanded.

"Audrey and I wanted to see how you're doing."

Horan calmed down. "Thanks for asking. I'm still not over what happened."

"The space flight or seeing Terrance Cogen's dead body?" Audrey jumped in.

Horan's eyes grew wide, and he looked like he was on the verge of a heart attack.

"What . . . what . . . ?" he managed.

"Mr. Cogen was murdered around the same time the ETs snatched you. A bit of a coincidence, no?" Audrey said.

"I . . . What are you suggesting?"

"I am suggesting that you made up that cock-and-bull story about an alien abduction to cover up your involvement in Terrance Cogen's murder."

"That's ridiculous."

"Not as ridiculous as your abduction story. We found your fingerprints in the living room in Dunthorpe near where his body was lying. How do you explain that?"

"I don't have to explain anything. I told you what happened. If this man was murdered when I was abducted, I have an alibi."

"You might have a problem producing witnesses to back it up," Audrey said.

"This conversation is over. I want you out of my house."

"Did you know Terrance Cogen?" Audrey asked.

"If you're not out of here immediately, I'm going to call Frank Curtin and your superiors."

"Do that. And while you're at it, tell them about your alibi."

Horan was sweating, and he was short of breath.

"Let's go, Audrey," Remington said. Then he turned to Horan. "Why don't you think about coming clean, Congressman. If you have a real alibi, we might be able to keep your involvement out of the papers."

Francine was waiting near the front door. "Did you get Tom to tell you what's bothering him?"

"No, but something has him terrified," Chad said. "If you can get him to open up, it might help him."

"Mrs. Horan, do you know Terrance Cogen?" Audrey asked.

"Of course. Tom and Terrance have known each other since high school, and he was one of Tom's closest friends. When I was working for Tom in DC, Terrance was a major campaign contributor. We were shocked when we learned that he was murdered. Why do you want to know?"

"He might have something to do with the people who kidnapped your husband."

"Why would Terrance do something like that?"

"We're not saying that he was involved, but the people who killed him may also have done something to your husband."

"Was Cogen helping your husband win his current campaign?" Chad asked.

"I think he was. I haven't been involved in the day-to-day running of the campaign since Tom and I married. You should talk to Eric Gilmore or Julie Sunderland. They're handling Tom's reelection campaign."

"Thanks for the information," Chad said. He started to walk out of the house.

Audrey started to follow him. Then she stopped and turned to Francine. "I don't think your husband has been entirely honest with us. I think he's hiding something that is terrifying him. Talk to him and see if you can get him to open up. We only want to help him, but we can't if he's not honest with us."

Audrey caught up to Chad as they walked to their car.

"Horan's fingerprints put him in the room where Cogen was killed, but he won't admit he was at Cogen's estate. There are two explanations for Horan's behavior. Horan killed Cogen, or he went to Cogen's house and found the body. If he found the body, why wouldn't he call 911?"

"If he killed Cogen, it would explain why he's terrified," Chad said. "If he's innocent, he might not have called 911 to avoid bad publicity. But there's a problem you haven't confronted. You can't date fingerprints, so we know Horan was in Cogen's living room, but we can't prove it was the day Cogen was murdered."

Remington shook his head. "There's something else going on here. I just don't have any idea what it is."

CHAPTER FIFTEEN

When Karen walked into the courtroom where Jack Blackburn was going to be arraigned, she noticed Muriel Lujack sitting in the back row and Oscar Vanderlasky seated at the prosecution table. Karen walked over to Vanderlasky while she waited for the guards to bring her client from the holding area.

"Hi, Oscar."

Vanderlasky looked up from his notes and flashed an insincere smile. "I've got your client dead to rights, Wyatt. Let me know when you're ready to discuss a plea."

"I'll do that," Karen said. Then she saw the guards leading Jack Blackburn out of the holding area, and she sat down at her counsel table.

"What's going to happen?" Blackburn asked when he was seated next to her. It was obvious that he was very nervous.

"Nothing much, today. The grand jury charged you with murder, car theft, and several other crimes in an indictment. Getting that document was necessary if the DA wanted to bring you to trial. We'll waive a reading of the indictment, and I'll enter a not guilty plea on your behalf. Then the judge will set a trial date. The date isn't binding. I'll probably be filing pretrial motions, so there will be a date set for them later. Meanwhile, my investigator is trying to find Billy Kramer and Cynthia Woodruff. It looks like they skipped town, but the DA is also looking for them, so there's a good chance they'll be found."

Before Karen could say anything more, the Honorable Nathan Stark took the bench. Stark was a no-nonsense former prosecutor who had been assigned to handle Blackburn's trial. Karen had tried one case in his court, and she had been happy with the way he had conducted the trial.

"This is the case of *State of Oregon v. Jack Thomas Blackburn*," the bailiff called.

Oscar Vanderlasky stood. "Ready for the State of Oregon."

"Ready for Mr. Blackburn," Karen said. "We will waive a reading of the indictment and enter a plea of not guilty. We would like to have the court set bail."

Vanderlasky smiled. "The State opposes bail. This is a murder case, so bail is not automatic."

"You know I can't set bail in a murder case without a hearing, Miss Wyatt," Judge Stark said. "Do you want to have me set one?"

"I do."

"Okay. I'll set a date for the hearing and trial. Court is adjourned."

Vanderlasky left the courtroom, and Karen told her client that she would be in touch soon. The spectator section had been packed, and Muriel Lujack was just getting into the aisle when Karen started for the courtroom door. Karen hadn't seen Muriel since the *Post* case, and she had not had a chance to talk to her one-on-one since the day she was freed from prison.

"Wait up, Muriel," Karen said.

Muriel froze in the middle of the aisle.

"Are you involved in Jack Blackburn's case?" Karen asked.

"No. I was just passing by."

Lujack looked nervous. Karen thought she might be uncomfortable because she had represented her office at Karen's hearing.

"I never got the chance to tell you how much I appreciated the way you handled my post-conviction hearing. I can think of some DAs who might have argued against my release."

"That would have been unethical," Muriel replied. "There was no question that you should never have been in prison."

"How are things going for you in the office? Did anyone hold what you did for me against you?"

"No. What happened to you was appalling. Most of the people in the office just wanted to forget it ever happened."

Karen noticed that Morris Johnson had entered the courtroom.

"Well, thanks," Karen said. Muriel flashed a nervous smile. When she left the courtroom, Johnson walked over to Karen.

"Mrs. Cogen is at the Westmont," Karen's investigator said.

"I talked to a bartender at the Clinton Street Tavern," Morris Johnson said as he drove Karen along the Willamette River. "He wasn't working the night that Kramer gave our client the Jag, and the waitress who served them is out of town at a funeral. I'll follow up, next week when they're back."

"Sounds good," Karen said moments before she spotted the stone pillars that marked the entrance to Portland's most exclusive country club. The tree-lined driveway passed the emerald-green fairway of the sixth hole of the club's championship golf course and ended at a sprawling fieldstone clubhouse that had started in 1925 as a small central building and grew larger and more imposing as Portland's rich and famous became members.

Karen had been taken to the Westmont by her own attorney, Harry Schmidt, who often entertained his well-to-do clients at the club. Karen was wealthy enough to afford the six figures it cost to become a member, but her drug-dealing, violent-offender clients weren't the types of people you wined and dined there.

It was a sunny day and close to lunchtime, so Karen led her investigator to a sprawling patio in the rear of the clubhouse, where she spotted Rosemarie Cogen eating a Caesar salad and sipping an iced tea under the shade of an umbrella.

"Mrs. Cogen, my name is Karen Wyatt. I'm an attorney, and this is my investigator, Morris Johnson. I'm sorry to bother you, but I'd be grateful if you could spare some time to talk to me."

Rosemarie studied Karen for a moment. Then her face lit up. "My, my, you're a celebrity, Miss Wyatt. I watched your press conference after you were sprung from the pokey. You look like you've coped quite well."

"It's been a few years, and I'm doing just fine."

"I bet the millions you got from those bastards who set you up must have helped."

"To be honest, no amount of money could ever make up for what I went through. But my settlement does give me the freedom to choose the people I want to represent without having to worry about the fee—people like Jack Blackburn, who is accused of killing your husband."

"I was not my husband's biggest fan, and I bear no ill will to the person who got him out of my life. Sit down. Can I get you or Mr. Johnson something to eat or drink?"

"Thanks, but we're good," Karen said as she took a seat that faced the eighteenth hole of the golf course, where a woman in a foursome was chipping onto the green. "Have you thought about anyone who might have had a sufficient motive to kill Mr. Cogen?"

"Not anyone in particular. I've been told that Terrance scammed a lot of people. An investigator said he looted the life savings of some of his victims. You might want to find the people he hurt. And there's Billy Kramer and Cynthia Woodruff—his chauffeur and maid. They've gone missing. I don't know why they would kill Terrance, but running away certainly makes them look guilty."

"Do you know if anything was stolen from the home?"

"You think robbery was the motive?"

"I'm just covering all the bases. My client swears that he's innocent."

"I haven't been back to the place since Terrance was murdered, so I don't know if anything is missing. Quite frankly, when he was alive, I didn't visit if I could help it. When I did, I never paid much attention to the décor."

Rosemarie shook her head. "Terrance had abominable taste. Any interior decorator who went into the living room would come out with PTSD. I do have jewelry in my bedroom. Some of it would bring a pretty penny, but, like I said, I haven't been back to my place to see if it's there.

"There are some valuable paintings. My grandfather was quite wealthy, and he hired a man named Hiram Ellington, who owned an art gallery, to purchase art for the mansion. There's a Turner seascape that the Tate has asked about and an early Cézanne in the living room. But Terrance and my father mucked up the room with African voodoo crap."

Rosemarie chuckled. "That statue that was used to brain Terrance was Rodin's *The Thinker*. From what I've been told, it's the real deal—a smaller version Rodin made as a model—but the killer probably figured it would be difficult to sell with blood and brains on it."

"You don't seem to be upset that Mr. Cogen was murdered."

"Is it that obvious?" Rosemarie sighed. "I guess I should try to appear upset, but I just didn't like Terrance."

"Did your husband shoot the taxidermied animals?"

"Heavens, no!" Rosemarie laughed. "Terrance wouldn't have had the guts to face down a lion. No, my father was the big-game hunter. He tried to get me interested in killing defenseless deer and rabbits, but I stopped hunting early on. It made me sick."

"There was an odd piece of information in the autopsy report," Karen said. "The medical examiner found traces of ice cream laced with a barbiturate in Mr. Cogen's stomach. It looks like the killer dosed him, then killed him when he was unconscious. Did your husband drink milkshakes?"

"Terrance was a recovering alcoholic. He guzzled milkshakes all the time to counter the urge to drink booze. That's why he got so fat." Rosemarie shuddered. "I found it repulsive."

"Who knew he drank milkshakes?" Karen asked.

"A lot of people. Billy Kramer and the chef used to make them, and Woodruff would know. So would anyone who socialized with Terrance."

Karen asked a few more questions before finishing her conversation with Rosemarie. She was walking across the patio toward the clubhouse when Oscar Vanderlasky walked out dressed in tennis whites and carrying a racket and a container of tennis balls. Vanderlasky looked surprised and stopped in front of Karen.

"You're not a member, are you?"

"No. I've been talking to Rosemarie Cogen."

Vanderlasky laughed. "The grieving widow. Did you get anything out of her?"

Karen smiled. "You'll find out when I send you discovery."

"Mrs. Cogen's testimony won't help you, Wyatt. Nothing will. And now I have to go." Vanderlasky puffed up his chest. "I'm in the semis of the club championship."

"Good luck," Karen said.

"I won't need it," Vanderlasky bragged as he strutted toward the tennis courts.

Morris shook his head. "What a tool."

"I'd say he's more of a blunt instrument," Karen commented.

CHAPTER SIXTEEN

An inheritance from his deceased parents had allowed Chad Remington to buy a condo in downtown Portland within walking distance of police headquarters that he wouldn't have been able to afford on his salary.

Chad was enjoying a pleasant dream in his king-size bed when the ringing of his phone woke him.

"Turn on Channel Six," Audrey said as soon as he picked up.

"What?" Chad asked, still groggy from being jerked out of a deep sleep.

"Channel Six. Turn it on now!"

Chad groped for his remote and pointed it at the set in his bedroom. When he switched to Channel Six, he saw a familiar face and Marlys Valentine, the host of *Wake Up, Portland*.

"Our guest this morning is Congressman Tom Horan, who

has an amazing story to tell everyone," Marlys told the television audience.

"Thanks for having me on, Marlys."

"It's always a pleasure. So, I understand you had quite an adventure recently."

"You don't think . . ." Chad said to his partner.

"Yes," Horan said, "but I wouldn't call what happened to me an *adventure*. It was the most terrifying and unsettling event I have ever experienced."

"Can you tell the audience and those watching at home what happened to you?"

Horan looked directly into the camera. Chad thought that the congressman was very nervous.

"This is difficult for me. As you know, Marlys, I'm running for a second term in the House of Representatives, and I'm absolutely certain that many voters are going to think I'm lying or—well, there's no other word that is more appropriate—insane. But I am willing to risk losing my election, because what I learned is more important than advancing my career."

"And what is this thing you learned?" the television host asked, trying so hard to keep her composure that Chad was certain that she knew what Horan was going to say.

"I learned that we are not alone in the universe, Marlys. Anyone who watched the House hearing on unidentified flying objects knows that I was the biggest skeptic on the committee, but I am a skeptic no longer." Horan paused for dramatic effect. "Several days ago, I was abducted by aliens."

Chad heard a gasp from the live studio audience.

"Were these aliens the 'little green men' we've heard so much about?" the host asked, trying successfully to keep a straight face.

"I don't blame you for being skeptical, Marlys. I know that

what I am saying is hard to believe. And no, they were huge and pale white, not green."

Chad watched open-mouthed while Horan told the audience the tale of his abduction.

"Why is he doing this?" he asked Audrey.

"Damned if I know, but I'd love to see his polling numbers when he's through spouting this cock-and-bull story."

"I'm not so sure this hurts him," Chad said. "You're way more rational than the voting public. A lot of people will buy into this because they want to believe we're not alone. Look at all the nonsense on social media that people think is real."

"I think he's shoring up his alibi, Chad. Horan must have been at Cogen's house. Either he killed him or he knows who did."

"Maybe so. But how do we prove it?"

"I think it's time we talked to Millie Horan."

Audrey Packer and Chad Remington found Millie at home in her seventh-floor condo in downtown Portland. The doorman had announced the detectives, and Millie was waiting at her door when they walked out of the elevator.

Millie Horan and her successor as Congressman Horan's wife were a study in contrasts. Francine Horan was the tall, leggy, blond stereotype of a trophy wife. Millie was barely over five feet tall with frizzy black hair, plain features, and no noticeable curves.

"Ralph said you are detectives," Millie said when Audrey and Chad reached her.

"Yes, ma'am," Chad said. "We're investigating a case in which Thomas Horan has a peripheral involvement."

Millie sneered. "What has Tom done now?"

"Can we step inside where your neighbors can't hear us?" Chad asked.

Millie ushered the detectives into her living room.

"Is Tom involved in a crime?" Millie asked when they were seated.

"We're not able to say that right now. But we would like to know about the congressman's relationship to Terrance Cogen."

"Do you think Tom killed Terrance?" Millie asked.

"We have nothing that points that way, but we would appreciate anything you can tell us about their relationship."

"It goes way back to high school. They were both on the chess team. That's where they met. Then the three of us ended up at the same college. That's where I met them."

"How did that happen?"

"Politics. Tom decided to run for class president, and Terrance was his hit man. They used every dirty trick in the book and won. I'm embarrassed to say that I was an aider and abettor."

Millie shook her head. "I was naïve and not very popular. Tom was the first boy who showed a real interest in me. I suspect that was because he couldn't get anyone else interested in him. But we were caught up in the thrill of winning the election. That's when we slept together for the first time, the night he won."

Millie sighed. She looked sad. "He did care for me back then. We were both poli-sci majors, and we were in the same classes. We studied together and moved in together. Everything was good even after we graduated. I went to law school, and he got a job with our state senator. By the time I graduated, Tom was the nominee for the statehouse in our district. He lost by a hair. The next time, he won. I was a senior associate in the Fields, Diez law firm. Being the wife of a politician on the rise didn't hurt. Then he won his congressional seat, moved to DC for most of the year, fell into the clutches of that bitch Francine, and that was that."

"After all the support you gave him, it must have been tough when you learned he was cheating on you," Audrey said sympathetically.

Millie looked directly at Audrey, her anger on display. "It was devastating at first, but I made Tom pay through the nose."

"There's a rumor that you forced his hand because you knew about financial improprieties that could have landed the congressman in hot water."

Millie's lips curled to form an evil smile. "When we divorced, I came out very well, but I also signed a nondisclosure agreement. If I breach it, I will take a massive hit financially, so I'm afraid I can't discuss anything involving Tom's finances."

"Can you tell us more about Mr. Horan's relationship to Terrance Cogen? Did it continue after college?"

"His legal contributions to Tom's campaigns are public record."

"Were there illegal contributions?" Audrey asked.

Millie's evil smile widened. "Like I said, I can't discuss my ex's financial arrangements."

"I'll take that as a yes," Audrey said.

Millie shrugged. "Take it any way you want to. Like they say, I can neither confirm nor deny."

"What about nonfinancial arrangements? This is not for public consumption. Can you keep a confidence?" Chad asked.

"I'm a lawyer. I know all about confidentiality."

"We found your husband's fingerprints in the room where we found Mr. Cogen's body."

"That doesn't surprise me. Terrance was one of Tom's closest friends."

"Was he involved in any shady business that had nothing to do with Mr. Horan?"

"I know he was being investigated for fraud. I was interviewed by a federal agent and an investigator from the district attorney's office, but I couldn't help them."

"Did Mr. Horan know that Mr. Cogen drank milkshakes?" Chad asked.

"What a peculiar question."

"It has a bearing on our investigation."

"Everyone who knew Terrance knew that. It was one of his more disgusting habits. When we were in college, he was thin and rather handsome. The last time I saw him, he was unflatteringly overweight. But I haven't seen Terrance since the divorce."

"Can you think of anything else that would help us?" Audrey asked.

"Since I don't know what you're after, except for questions about Tom's finances, I can't."

The detectives talked to Millie a little longer. Then they thanked her and left. Audrey and Chad waited until they were on the street to talk about the interview.

"What did you think about the ex–Mrs. Horan?" Audrey asked.

"I think that she is royally pissed at her ex and would have gladly told us anything negative about him, if she could."

"Agreed. And I'm certain that she would gladly do her husband and the deceased a lot of damage if we could find a way to get around that nondisclosure agreement."

CHAPTER SEVENTEEN

Thomas Horan's campaign headquarters was located in a storefront office in the heart of the district he represented. Volunteers manned phone lines that seemed to be ringing nonstop, and everyone in the campaign headquarters looked distracted and stressed. The volunteers were supervised by a middle-aged woman who looked like she was an inch away from a nervous breakdown.

"Are you Julie Sunderland?" Audrey Packer asked.

"I am, but I'm too busy to talk if you're with the press."

"Damage control?" Audrey guessed.

"If you want a comment, you'll have to wait for the congressman to hold a press conference."

Audrey showed her credentials so only Sunderland could see them.

"I'm not a reporter," she said quietly so that she wouldn't be overheard. "I'm a homicide detective. Do you have somewhere private where we can talk? After Representative Horan's tale of his space adventure, I can't imagine you want any more stories floating about."

Sunderland was clearly flustered. "Yes, certainly," she said. "Let's go to my office."

Moments later, the women were seated in a claustrophobic office crowded with filing cabinets, a desk dominated by a computer monitor and piled high with campaign literature, and a wall covered with pictures of Thomas Horan shaking hands with the president, generals, and celebrities.

"I imagine your phone has been ringing like crazy ever since the congressman's television appearance," Audrey said as soon as the door was closed.

"Can you please get to the point? It's been a madhouse, and I don't have time for chitchat. What's this about?"

"Was Terrance Cogen's connection to Congressman Horan strictly as a donor to his campaign, or were they friends?"

"Does this have something to do with Mr. Cogen's murder?"

"We're just gathering background information," Audrey answered.

"Mr. Cogen did contribute to Tom's campaign, and he attended some of our fundraisers. They also socialized. The congressman has been friends with Mr. Cogen since high school."

"Was Mr. Cogen a major contributor?"

"He did give the maximum that is allowed legally."

"Just out of curiosity—and it won't go any further—what's been the reaction to the congressman's TV appearance?"

Sunderland closed her eyes, tilted her head back, and took a deep breath.

"It's been utter chaos in here. If he'd asked Eric or me about going on that show . . . I don't know what Tom was thinking."

"So, the reaction has been negative?"

Sunderland pursed her lips and her brow furrowed. "It's been weird, but it hasn't been all bad. We've had a lot of calls applauding Tom's courage and making donations to his campaign. We've also had some donors asking for their money back. It's too early to say, but right now, I'd say it's a push."

"Thanks for your help, Miss Sunderland. Is there anyone else I can talk to who might know more about the congressman's relationship to Mr. Cogen?"

"You don't think Tom had any involvement in Mr. Cogen's death, do you?"

"We don't have any evidence pointing that way. Like I said, this is just background."

"Have you talked to Tom's wife, Francine?"

"She's the one who suggested I talk to you."

"Eric might know something."

"Eric Gilmore?"

"Yes, but he's in Washington right now."

"Do you have a phone number I can use to reach him?"

Audrey wrote down the number and left. Terrance Cogen had stolen a lot of money, and no one knew what had happened to it. Audrey wondered if some of it had been washed through Thomas Horan's campaign.

While Audrey Packer was interviewing Julie Sunderland at Thomas Horan's election headquarters, Chad Remington was eating lunch with Sol Krieger, an old acquaintance, at a Chinese restaurant a few blocks north of the federal building, where Krieger prosecuted financial crimes.

"Why are you springing for my General Tso's chicken," Krieger asked as soon as the waitress took their order.

"I was assigned the Terrance Cogen case, and I understand you were looking into his scams."

"I was, and I still am."

"What can you tell me?"

"Mr. Cogen was involved in a lot of bad shit. Have you been to his penthouse?"

"I have. And Mrs. Cogen told me it wasn't his. She said that she owns the penthouse and the estate."

Krieger smiled. "Rosemarie is one sexy woman, and way smarter than Terrance." He shook his head. "I have no idea what she saw in him."

"I saw some pictures before he put on all that weight. He was a good-looking guy, and he must be a smooth talker to pull off all those scams."

"Everything he did was very stupid. There's no question that he was going to be caught eventually." Krieger shook his head. "A lady with her IQ should have seen through him. Did you know she was a math major at Stanford?"

"No."

"She belongs to Mensa and used to be a rated chess player. And if you thought she was a trust fund baby, you would be wrong. She didn't inherit much beyond the Dunthorpe place from her father. She made her dough through the stock market, and she did very nicely."

"What was Cogen doing?"

"I'll get you my reports so you can see the details, but he stole a lot of money from the condo after he got himself elected as the condo's treasurer. There were unaccounted millions that were supposed to go to building projects that never happened.

"Another scam involved apartment complexes he was supposedly building. He would dupe people into investing in them. Then he would forge the investors' signatures, secretly sell the properties, and pocket the profits. Some investors put their entire retirement accounts into his scheme.

"His stupidest scam involved borrowing money from banks,

then forging documents that said he'd paid back the loan so he could get another loan from another bank."

Krieger shook his head again. "It's one thing to steal from your HOA or retirees, but you do not fuck with banks. They were the first to figure out what was going on. We started looking into the bank scams, and one thing led to another."

"It sounds like he was stealing a lot of money," Chad said.

"It was in the millions."

"Has the money been recovered?"

"We're searching for it."

"Do you think he was acting alone?"

"No way. He wasn't smart enough to figure out how to hide his ill-gotten gains. We're pretty sure that he was laundering money through the Lucifer's Disciples, but we don't have enough to go after them yet."

"Do you think Mrs. Cogen was involved? From what you've said, she would know how to hide the money."

"It's possible, but we don't have any evidence that points to her."

Their food came. Chad and Krieger talked about Cogen some more, then switched to sports and their private lives. Chad said goodbye and started walking back to police headquarters when his phone rang. He answered it and learned that they had gotten a hit on Cynthia Woodruff's car.

CHAPTER EIGHTEEN

Billy Kramer had an orgasm and collapsed on top of Cynthia Woodruff. Woodruff waited a while. When Billy's weight got to be too much, she shoved him off and stood up.

"You still got it, Cyn," Kramer said.

Cynthia was fed up. She wanted to say that all she had was a sore pussy, but she kept that thought to herself. When she was dressed, she weaved her way through a maze of pizza boxes and take-out Thai and headed for the door to their motel room.

"Where are you going?" Kramer asked.

"Out. We've been stuck in this room for two days. I've got to get some fresh air or I'll go stir-crazy."

Kramer stood up and walked over to Woodruff. "You can't go out, babe. It's too dangerous."

"What's going on, Billy? First you tell me to take that guy to the Jag. Then you tell me we have to leave Oregon. And every time I ask you to explain something, all you tell me is that we're in trouble. As far as I can see, I'm not in any trouble. If you are, I don't want any part of it."

"Well, you are part of it, whether you want to be or not."

"Part of what? Either you tell me right now or I'm out of here."

"Terrance is dead, murdered."

"What?"

"Someone beat his head in."

"Was it you, Billy? Is that why you're running?"

"Hey, Cyn, how can you think that?"

"I don't know, Billy. Maybe it's because you're hiding in a fleabag motel in bumfuck Arizona."

Billy put his hands on Cynthia's shoulders. Then he looked her in the eyes. "You know me, Cyn. Do you honestly believe I could kill Cogen?"

Cynthia broke eye contact and pulled away. "The way you're acting, I don't know what to think."

"Jesus, Cyn. I love you. You don't lie to someone you love."

"You had me lie to that guy to get him to take the Jag. Were you setting him up?"

Billy gave a nervous laugh. "Jack will be fine. If he gets picked up, he'll just tell the cops what happened."

"Why would he get picked up? What did you do?"

"I was protecting us."

"How, Billy?"

Kramer looked down. "I reported the car stolen."

"You what?!"

"If they think Jack stole the car, they'll think he killed Cogen, and it will take the heat off of us."

"That was a rotten thing to do."

"I won't let it get too far. I'll clear his name if I see that he's in danger of being convicted for something."

"You think the cops will believe you? If Cogen is dead and you've run away, they'll think you killed him. And they'll think I'm involved because I ran with you. How could you do this to me?"

"I'm sorry, Cyn. I needed you to set up Jack. I couldn't think of any other way to do it."

"That's the problem, Billy. You never think of anyone but yourself."

Cynthia walked over to her suitcase and opened it.

"What are you doing?"

"I'm going back to Portland. If the cops question me, I'm going to tell them everything I know."

"You can't do that."

"Watch me."

"There's another problem. It has nothing to do with the cops."

Cynthia stopped packing and turned to face Kramer. "What other problem?"

Kramer licked his lips. "You know Cogen was involved in some shady stuff?"

"Yeah. You hinted at that, but you never told me what he was doing."

"He stole money, Cyn, a lot of money, and he had to clean it so he could use it. I was helping him launder the dough through legit businesses."

"What does that have to do with me?"

"Some of the businesses are owned by the Disciples."

"Oh no, Billy. They're maniacs. How could you get involved with them?"

"Walt Zegda and I go way back. We've been friends since high school. That's why I told Cogen about his garages."

"If you're his friend, why are you worried?"

"It's his personality, Cyn. It ain't normal. He can be your best buddy one minute, stab you the next, and eat a plate of spaghetti smothered in tomato sauce while you're bleeding out."

"That's disgusting."

"It's also the way he is. If he worries that I'll tell the cops about laundering Cogen's cash through his businesses, he'll see me as a liability, and that will be that."

"I didn't have anything to do with money laundering."

"I know that, but Walt might not want to take any chances."

Cynthia's hands curled into fists, and her face turned red with rage. "You thoughtless bastard. You're telling me that the alternatives to staying in this fucking room are being charged with murder or being killed by your psychopathic buddy?"

"That sums it up, Cyn. We have to stay under the radar until the cops figure out who killed Cogen."

Cynthia turned away from Billy and paced back and forth. "I don't believe this," she said.

"I'm sorry, Cyn."

"*Sorry* doesn't cut it. And I'm serious about getting out of this room. I can't take it anymore. Can't we go to that tavern we saw when we pulled in? It's only half a block away."

"I don't know . . ."

Cynthia put her arms around Billy's neck and pressed her body against his.

"Please, baby." She kissed Billy and ground her crotch against his. "I'll make it worth your while when we get back."

Whenever he was aroused, Billy's brain switched off. Moments after a deep kiss, he was getting dressed and following Cynthia into the warm night air.

"Bingo!" Wolf Larson said to Walter Zegda, who was working his Rubik's Cube while he watched a crew of Disciples packaging heroin from the latest shipment.

Zegda stopped playing with his toy. "What's got you so excited?"

"Kramer is in a small town in Arizona. One of our guys saw him and a woman eating dinner at a bar and followed them to a motel."

"I want them picked up pronto and brought here in one piece. Tell our boys I'll show my appreciation."

"I'm on it," Wolf said.

Zegda felt sad. He and Billy went way back. He hoped he wouldn't have to kill him.

CHAPTER NINETEEN

Carl Ridley had swapped his Harley for a dull brown van with a logo for a plumbing company that did not exist. Instead of his Lucifer's Disciples colors, he was wearing jeans, a flannel shirt, steel-toed boots, and a gray hoodie. The four other members of the Disciples' Arizona affiliate were also in civilian dress. Everyone was armed.

"They're in room twenty-four on the second floor of the motel," Carl said to his men, who were standing next to the van in the darkened garage. "Walter wants them alive, so no rough stuff unless it is absolutely necessary. I'll take the lead when we get there. Any questions?"

No one had any, so Carl sat in the passenger seat next to his driver, and everyone else piled into the back of the van. Carl went over the plan during the ride to the motel. It would be shock and awe. Threaten the clerk and get the room key. Open the door, scare the shit out of Kramer and his girlfriend, hustle them down to the van, quick in, quick out. He couldn't see how the plan could go wrong, until the van drew even with the entrance to the motel parking lot and he saw the police cars. There were four of them, and many of their occupants were standing in the open door of room 24.

Walter's not going to like this, Carl thought just before he told his driver to drive away slowly so they didn't attract attention.

Audrey Packer and Chad Remington were exhausted and hungry after the hurried flight to Arizona and the drive to Red Rim. They ate a fast meal and drank several cups of coffee at a café before walking two blocks to the police station and introducing themselves to the police chief.

The police station in Red Rim looked like it hadn't been updated since the Earp brothers were the law in the Wild West. The interrogation room where Chad was meeting with Billy Kramer was dim and uncomfortably hot and smelled of stale coffee and sweat. Chad was sitting in a cushioned chair across from Billy Kramer, whose butt was pressed against a hard metal seat. The locals had roughed up Kramer when they'd made the arrest, and there was a bruise under his left eye.

"Can I call you Billy?" Remington asked after introducing himself.

"You can call my lawyer," Kramer responded.

Chad smiled. "You're not under arrest, Billy. You could be, because you stole Terrance Cogen's Jag, but you don't have to be, if you tell me what you know about your boss's murder."

"I don't know anything about that."

"Then why are you hiding in a small town in Arizona?"

Kramer leaned back, stared at Chad, and folded his arms across his chest. "I'm on vacation."

"I don't want to spoil your time off, so why don't you cooperate?"

"And put my head in a noose? I know you're trying to frame me for murder, and I know you can't ask me questions as soon as I ask for a lawyer."

Next door, Audrey Packer was having a lot more luck with Cynthia Woodruff. She had given Kramer's girlfriend her Miranda rights, but Cynthia had waived them, claiming that she didn't need a lawyer because she "hadn't done a damn thing, except let that bastard Billy drag me into this mess."

Audrey could see how a woman like Cynthia could fall for a handsome fast-talker like Kramer. Terrance Cogen's chauffeur had the good looks and glib tongue of a con man, and Cynthia had the plain looks and chubby body of a woman who never expected that someone like Kramer would be interested in her. But Audrey discovered very quickly that Cynthia wasn't stupid and that any hold Kramer might have had on her had been ripped off as soon as her arrest had opened her eyes.

"This is all on Billy," Cynthia said. "I don't know anything about Mr. Cogen's murder."

"What has Billy got to do with you hiding in Red Rim?" Audrey asked.

"Everything."

"Why don't you explain that to me."

Cynthia was angry, and she was about to tell Audrey everything, when a thought occurred to her. "Am I in trouble?"

"That depends on what you've done."

Cynthia leaned forward and looked directly at Audrey. "I haven't done a damn thing, except what Billy tricked me into."

"Cynthia, you haven't told me what Billy did. I can't decide whether you're in trouble if I don't have any facts."

Cynthia leaned back and looked down. Audrey let her think. Eventually, Cynthia sat up.

"Okay. I'll tell you what happened. First of all, I didn't even know that Mr. Cogen was dead until Billy told me yesterday."

"Did Billy tell you he killed him?"

"No. He said he didn't."

"Do you believe him?"

"I don't know what to believe. Billy has no trouble lying. I do know he set up that guy Jack."

"Oh? How did he do that?"

"It's how I got in this mess. Billy called and said he needed a favor. He said he wanted me to pack for a surprise vacation and drive my car to this bar. I said I was eating dinner, but he said he was taking me somewhere special once I did him this favor. I asked him why he needed my car if he was taking me on a vacation. He told me he'd explain when I got to the bar."

Cynthia sighed. "Billy can be sweet when he wants to be, and we'd been seeing each other. He got me believing it was serious, although I'm not so sure now."

"What happened at the bar?" Audrey asked to get Cynthia back on track.

"He asked for my car keys."

"Why did he want you to give him your car keys?"

"So he could pick me up later. The idea was I was going to be with Billy when this Jack showed up at the bar. After a while, I was supposed to say that I wanted to go home. Billy was going to say he was too drunk to drive and Jack should drive me in the Jag.

"Billy told me that Jack was crazy about cars and would go nuts about being able to drive the Jag. I asked him what he was doing with the Jag. I don't know anything about cars, but I knew that this Jag was very expensive and Mr. Cogen's pride and joy. Billy said Mr. Cogen had said he could use it.

"A little while after I got to the bar, Jack came in. About half an hour later, Billy gave me the signal. I said I wanted to go home, Billy said he was too drunk to drive, and I took Jack to the Jag. He was out of his mind as soon as he saw the car, and he couldn't wait to drop me off. I sent him to a part of town far from my apartment. It was where Billy said he'd be, but he wasn't waiting for me. Jack drove off, and I started to worry. I texted Billy, and he said to hold on, that he was on the way. About an hour later, Billy picked me up in my car, and we drove here."

"Why did Billy want Jack to drive the Jag?" Audrey asked.

Cynthia shook her head. "That was the worst thing Billy did. That's when I knew I had to get away from him."

"Can you explain that to me?"

"He's trying to frame this guy Jack for Mr. Cogen's murder."

"How did giving him the Jag do that?" Audrey asked, even though she knew the answer.

"The bastard called the cops and said that the Jag was stolen. He figured that the cops would think Jack killed Mr. Cogen when he stole the Jag. I told Billy it was a rotten thing to do. He said he'd clear everything up with the cops if Jack got in a lot of trouble, but I don't believe him."

"Did Billy say anything about bringing a beer glass to Mr. Cogen's house?"

"A beer glass?"

"From the bar where you met Jack."

"I don't remember him saying anything about a beer glass. Is it important?"

"It's just something that came up. Don't worry about it. Is there anything else you want to tell me?" Audrey asked.

Cynthia remembered what Billy had said about his and Terrance Cogen's connection to the Lucifer's Disciples, but she was more frightened of the Disciples than she was of the police.

"No, that's it."

"You've really helped yourself, Cynthia."

"What's going to happen to me?"

"You've given me a lot to think about," Audrey said.

"Are you going to let me go? I didn't do anything wrong."

"I'm leaning that way, but I want to talk to my partner. Would you be willing to tell a district attorney what you told me?"

"Yeah, if you promised that I wouldn't get charged."

"Are you hungry?" Audrey asked.

"Yeah."

"I'm going to have a meal brought to you while I talk to my partner. I'll also see if there's somewhere more comfortable for you to stay. Hang tight while I figure out how to help you."

Chad was sitting on a bench sipping a cup of coffee outside the room where Audrey was talking to Cynthia Woodruff. He stood up when Audrey walked into the hall.

"Any luck?" Audrey asked.

Chad shook his head. "My guy stonewalled. What about you?"

"Cynthia is really pissed off at Mr. Kramer," Audrey said before telling her partner everything she'd learned from Woodruff. "What do you want to do with Kramer?" Audrey asked when she was through.

"They're arranging for him to talk to a lawyer. He's coming over in the morning, so we're in limbo until they conference. What do you want to do with Woodruff?"

"I think she'll come back to Portland with us. I'll want to get her immunity from prosecution if she agrees to testify against Kramer. She's mad enough at him, so I think she'll agree."

"Do we have a problem with the charges against Jack Blackburn?" Chad asked.

"That's up to Oscar Vanderlasky to decide. But Cynthia is going to supply Karen Wyatt with a treasure trove of reasonable doubts."

CHAPTER TWENTY

Karen Wyatt had been to the theater with Barry Clay, a doctor who had been an expert witness in a case she had tried several months earlier. They had spent a lot of time together when she was preparing his testimony, and he had asked her out after the trial ended. She liked going out with Barry because he was funny and kind, and he had his own successful career, so she didn't worry about her money motivating his interest.

Karen and the doctor had gone to a club to hear a local singer after the theater, and she hadn't gotten to bed until two in the morning. She was bleary-eyed when she got to the office and was having trouble tracking the facts in a dense opinion in a complicated probate case she was handling. When Morris Johnson walked into her office, she was grateful for the interruption.

"A little birdie just told me that Billy Kramer and Cynthia Woodruff are back in Portland and that Woodruff is cooperating with the DA," the investigator said.

"Who is this miniature avian?"

"Uh-uh. I still have friends in the PPB, and their identities are on a need-to-know basis."

"Why haven't we gotten discovery?"

"Maybe it's because Oscar Vanderlasky has the case?"

Karen pulled out her phone, set it on speaker, and dialed Vanderlasky.

"Hi, Oscar. I hear Cynthia Woodruff is back in town and assisting your investigation."

"Where did you hear that?" Vanderlasky demanded.

"I have my sources. Anyway, since I know you're a stickler for following the rules of criminal procedure, I assume you've got a bunch of police reports that set out what Miss Woodruff and Mr. Kramer have told you. Can I send my investigator over to your office to pick them up, or are you going to messenger them to me?"

"When I have discovery for you, I'll let you know," Vanderlasky said, barely able to contain his anger.

"I'm not going to have to waste our valuable time filing a motion with Judge Stark, am I?"

"Do what you want, Wyatt. You'll get discovery when I'm ready to give it to you."

Karen disconnected and smiled. "I'm guessing we'll get the reports sometime tomorrow."

When Jack Blackburn walked into the contact visiting room, Karen thought that he looked worse than the last time she'd been with him. He had been slim. Now he looked emaciated, his shoulders slumped, there were dark circles under his eyes, and he gave Karen the impression that the short walk from the door to his seat across the table from her had used up all of his energy.

"How are you doing?" she asked, concerned by her client's deterioration.

"It's tough in here. I'm not sleeping, and I'm scared."

"Then I have some news that might cheer you up. Billy Kramer and Cynthia Woodruff were arrested in Arizona, and they're back in Portland. Kramer isn't talking, but Woodruff has an immunity deal, and she's told the detectives and the DA some things that help your case."

Jack sat up straight. "What did she say?"

"She explained that Billy set you up with the Jag. Then he called the cops and told them you stole it. I'm sure that the DA was going to argue that you killed Mr. Cogen when you were stealing his car. Woodruff's testimony proves that you didn't steal the car. Billy gave it to you. If we can show that you didn't steal the Jag, your motive for murder disappears."

It took a few seconds for Blackburn to digest what Karen had just told him. Then his eyes teared up.

"Thank you, Miss Wyatt. You're the first person who ever stood up for me. No one else has ever done that, and I want to thank you."

Karen's eyes started to tear up too. She squeezed Jack's hand.

"I'm going to do my best to get you out of this mess. Just hang in there." She stood up. "I'm going to talk to the DA who has your case. I'll let you know what I find out. Keep your fingers crossed."

The first thing Karen noticed when she walked into Oscar Vanderlasky's office was his wall of fame decorated with framed clippings from his best wins as a lawyer and as a tennis player.

Under the framed clippings was a bookcase. Trophies and awards attesting to his superiority in law and athletics cluttered its top.

"Nice trophies," Karen said.

Oscar leaned back in his chair and greeted Karen with a smug smile. "I earned every one of them, and I'm going to add another headline soon."

Karen sat across from Vanderlasky. "I hope you're not talking about the murder charge."

"I am—and every other charge in the indictment."

"How do you figure that, after talking to Cynthia Woodruff?"

Vanderlasky shook his head slowly. "Karen, I'm surprised. You're usually so sharp, but you don't appear to have a grasp of the facts. Your client may have gotten the Jaguar from Billy Kramer, but he knew who really owned it, because Terrance Cogen's name and address are on the registration. Does Blackburn drive the car to Cogen's estate to return it? I say he does, but Billy has disappeared and Cogen accuses Jack of stealing his car. Maybe he asks Jack in to get him to confess. Who knows? What we do know is Jack and Terrance have a beer and a milkshake together. Jack poisons the shake, then bashes in Cogen's head when he passes out. What's his motive? We know from Cynthia that he is in love with the Jag. He can't give back his dream car, so he kills its legal owner so he can keep it."

"That makes no sense, Oscar. If he drives to Cogen's estate looking for Billy Kramer, why would he have poison with him? And how in the world would he ever be able to keep that car? A guy like Jack? Every time he took it out, it would be like he was trailing a neon sign with the word *STOLEN* on it."

Vanderlasky shrugged. "Ask your client to answer your questions. The fingerprints on the beer glass are going to send Mr. Blackburn to OSP."

Karen stood up. "I hope you change your mind when you've

given this case more thought. I'd entertain a plea to auto theft if you drop the murder charge."

Vanderlasky smiled. "Nice try, Karen, but your boy is going down."

Karen walked out of Vanderlasky's office, afraid of what she might say to the conceited bastard if she stayed any longer. Then her anger drained away, and she felt sick about what she was going to have to tell Jack Blackburn after she'd foolishly built up his hopes.

When she calmed down, she ran through Vanderlasky's argument. The key was the beer glass with Jack's prints on it that placed him at the murder scene. She smiled. There was no doubt in her mind that Billy Kramer took that glass from the bar where he'd met Jack and carried it to Cogen's house. If she could get Kramer to admit what he'd done, Vanderlasky's case would fall apart.

Her smile morphed into a frown. How was she going to get Kramer to admit that he'd planted the beer glass? The only reason he would have done that was if he knew Cogen was dead in his living room, and he would only know that if he'd seen the body. That could have happened if Kramer murdered his boss or found the body after someone else killed him, which created a problem. If Kramer didn't kill Terrance Cogen, he would supply the police with overwhelming evidence that he did, if he confessed to planting the glass and tricking Jack Blackburn into taking the Jag to frame Blackburn for the killing.

How could she get Kramer to confess to planting the glass when that confession would put a noose around his neck? That was the question.

CHAPTER TWENTY-ONE

Gabby Wright was sitting at a table in the back of the Lucifer's Disciples' clubhouse with five other gang members. He was holding three sevens and was deciding whether to raise after another Disciple had just raised him when his cell phone started playing "Bad to the Bone," his ring tone. Gabby glanced at the caller ID and saw Walter Zegda's name.

"Hold on a sec, Walt," Gabby said. "Felix and me are doing battle."

Felix was a terrible poker player, and Gabby was certain he was bluffing.

"I'll raise, Felix," Gabby said.

Felix stared at the pot, hesitated, then called.

Gabby laid down his cards, and Felix swore. Gabby pocketed

his winnings and walked to a place where he could talk to Zegda without being overheard.

"What's up?" Gabby said.

"I have a job for you. There's a deputy DA I want you to follow. I'll text you her picture. Let me know what she does and who she meets. Just shadow her. Don't make contact."

Gabby disconnected. Moments later, Zegda sent him a photo of Muriel Lujack.

Muriel Lujack closed her eyes and sighed. Two hours ago, her jury had brought in a guilty verdict in a sex abuse case that she was not sure she was going to win. Adrenaline had kept her going while she was in trial, but that stimulant had disappeared as fast as bathwater swirling down a drain as soon as she closed the door to her office, leaving her completely exhausted.

The smart thing to do would have been to go home and veg out, but Muriel was genetically programmed to be conscientious, so she had worked up her case summary and notes about possible appellate issues as soon as she was in her office, a task she'd just finished.

Muriel was about to go home when the door opened and Ellen Kaufman walked in with a big smile on her face.

"Congratulations! The detectives just told me that you won *Foster*. You must be over the moon."

Muriel gave her boss a tired smile. "I'm just relieved."

"The detectives said you were terrific. They thought your closing argument nailed it."

"I'm glad they liked it."

"Hey, don't go all modest on me. There are several attorneys in this office—who I will not name—who I don't think could have pulled this off."

"Thanks for the vote of confidence. I'm going to go home and celebrate by taking a hot bath and going to bed."

Ellen laughed. Then she looked serious. "There was something I wanted to ask you. Whenever someone checks out a closed case file, everyone gets a text from the clerk."

Muriel felt a jolt of fear. "Why does that happen?"

"If someone else in the office knows about the case, they might be able to help," Kaufman answered. "Anyway, I understand that you've been looking into old files about the *Baer* case. Is there something I can help you with?"

"Why do you care that I was reading those files?"

"Come on, Muriel. You handled Karen Wyatt's post-conviction hearing. The *Baer* case and its aftermath were devastating for this office and the PPB. And it was personal for me. I mentored Donna Ridley." She shook her head. "When I found out that she was being bribed by the Disciples, I felt like a complete failure. So, I'm asking you: Why were you looking at the files? Because I want to know if there was something we missed, like another person who was also on the take."

Muriel tried to fight through her fatigue and think about her answer. She didn't know who she could trust, so she lied.

"Ever since I handled Wyatt's case, I've been intrigued by what happened as a result of the raid on the Demon Slayers, so I've been reading up on it to try to get a handle on what happened. So far, I haven't found anything that everyone else doesn't know. If I do find anything, I'll definitely tell you."

"Thanks, Muriel. There's one more reason I wanted to talk to you. How much do you know about Terrance Cogen's murder?"

"Not much. Mostly what I've read in the paper."

"We've charged a person named Jack Blackburn with the crime. Oscar Vanderlasky has the case. Billy Kramer and Cynthia Woodruff worked as Cogen's chauffeur and maid. They disappeared right around the time that Cogen was murdered, and we just found them hiding out in Arizona. They're back in Portland. Woodruff has immunity and is cooperating, but Billy Kramer lawyered up. I want you to handle his case."

"Is it a murder case? I don't have the experience to handle a homicide."

"I know that. The situation is confusing, because Kramer may or may not be involved in the murder. You're basically going to be a placeholder while we figure out what we want to do. If we decide to charge Kramer with murder, I'll substitute someone in, and you can ride shotgun. It will be good experience for when you get your own homicide cases. Is that okay?"

"I guess."

"I'm giving you this case to show you what I think of your talent. Keep up the good work. You have a real future in this office."

The door closed behind Ellen. Muriel was thrilled that her supervisor thought enough of her to give her the *Kramer* case, but Kaufman's questions about the *Baer* case had unnerved her. She didn't know that the clerk notified everyone in the office when a closed case was taken from the files. That meant that the traitor in the DA's office knew that she was looking into the case.

Muriel was too tired to think clearly. She grabbed her coat and left the office. It usually took her twenty-five minutes to walk to her apartment. She was sitting at a desk or in court most of every day, so walking to and from her apartment was usually the only exercise she got during the week.

There was a chill in the night air, and Muriel turned up her collar to ward off the cold wind that was racing down the streets that led from the river. At this hour, there were few people on the streets. Most of downtown was well lighted, but there were short stretches that were cast in shadow. She was still spooked by her conversation with Ellen about the *Baer* case, and she couldn't help looking over her shoulder or peering into the dark spaces whenever a sound on the deserted streets startled her.

She was just crossing Burnside to go from the Southwest area of the city to the Northwest when the clank of a can rolling along the street brought her up short. She turned toward the sound. There was someone in a doorway at the end of the street. Was it a homeless person seeking shelter or someone following her?

Powell's City of Books, Portland's world-famous bookstore, took up a block. There was a reading tonight, and she hurried across the street to mix with the crowd. She turned at the entrance and looked down the street. There were people at the crosswalk, but no one who looked suspicious.

Muriel worked her way through the store and left by a back entrance. She had five more blocks to navigate before she was home, but there were loading docks for warehouses on some of them and very little foot traffic. One street boasted two popular restaurants, and she angled toward them, casting glances over her shoulder as she went.

Her heart was racing by the time she arrived at the front door of her apartment house. It was on a poorly lighted side street, and there was no one walking along it. Muriel saw a man standing in the shadows at the end of the street she had just crossed. Was he staring at her? He was shrouded in shadow and too far away for her to tell. Her hand shook as she tried to fit her key in the front door. Once she was in the lobby with the door shut behind her, she tried to calm down.

When she was inside her apartment, she locked the door but didn't turn on the lights. She peered through the window that looked out on the front of her building. When she didn't see anyone lurking on the street, she squeezed her eyes shut and took a deep breath. Had someone really followed her, or was her stalker a product of her overactive imagination?

Muriel turned on her lights. She put the teakettle on to boil and fixed dinner. She was reading a good novel, and she distracted herself by getting into it while she ate. After dinner, she took a hot bath and went to bed. The warmth of the bath had soaked out a lot of her tension, but thoughts started to swirl when she was under her covers, and it took a while before she could banish them and fall asleep.

CHAPTER TWENTY-TWO

By the time Muriel got to her office the next morning, she had decided that she was at a dead end. She'd reviewed every case involving the Lucifer's Disciples to see if there was something that pointed at a specific DA who could have been involved in the plot to frame Karen Wyatt. She had found a few cases that had been dismissed because evidence had gone missing or a key witness had disappeared, but different prosecutors on her list of suspects had been assigned to the cases, and she couldn't find a pattern involving only one DA.

At lunchtime, Muriel left the courthouse and waited until she was a few blocks away before making a call that she hoped was not a mistake.

"Karen Wyatt and Associates," the receptionist said.

"I'd like to talk to Miss Wyatt."

"Who shall I say is calling?"

"I'm a potential client."

When Karen picked up, Muriel said, "Miss Wyatt, this is Muriel Lujack."

"My receptionist said you're a possible client?"

"I didn't want to give her my name."

"Is this about a case? I didn't think anyone in my office had one with you."

"You don't. This is personal. Can we meet after work, someplace where no one will see us?"

There was dead air for a moment. Then Karen asked, "Are you in trouble?"

"This is about you and the people who set you up. I don't want to say any more until we meet."

Muriel and Karen chose a restaurant in Sandy, Oregon, a town that was twenty miles from Portland. The restaurant served good Italian food, but neither woman had much of an appetite.

"What's this all about?" Karen asked as soon as the waiter left with their orders.

"I had a visitor who is a friend of a person I'm prosecuting. She wanted to know if I'd give him a break if she told me something important about a big case. It was your case."

Without mentioning names, Muriel gave Karen the gist of what Nikki Randolph had told her. Then Muriel handed Karen the list of suspects she had compiled.

"I've scoured the files of cases handled by the DAs who were around when you were set up, but I haven't found anything that makes me suspect any particular prosecutor."

"Why are you telling me this?" Karen asked.

"I've hit a brick wall, and I don't feel comfortable investigating the people I work with anymore. If my information is correct, one of these people deserves to be in prison. They may be betraying their oath of office every day. I need to know if there is a traitor in the DA's office, but I don't have the means to find out. You do. You've got investigators, money, everything you need to expose this person."

Karen digested what Muriel had told her, and Muriel waited for Karen's answer.

"I appreciate what you've done. It can't have been easy. I'm going to use what you've told me. I just don't know how right now."

"When you figure that out, don't tell me. If the person you're looking for finds out I'm involved, I won't be safe."

Muriel left while Karen paid the bill so they wouldn't be seen together. Karen was deep in thought all the way home. Finding the traitor in the DA's office required an investigator, and she employed one of the best. During the drive, she called Morris Johnson and told him to meet her at her apartment.

Gabby Wright had earned his nickname because he rarely spoke. He was also the first person that Walter Zegda relied on if he wanted someone followed because he was average height, slender, with average looks. In other words, the type of person no one notices.

Gabby followed Muriel Lujack to the Italian restaurant in Sandy, Oregon, and watched the place from the shadows of a parking lot across the street. He texted Zegda when Karen Wyatt joined her. Gabby knew who Wyatt was because all the Disciples knew about the *Baer* case and its aftermath.

Zegda told Gabby to go home now that he had some idea of what Lujack was up to. What he hadn't decided was what he should do about it. Snuffing a DA was a last resort because it would bring down so much heat that it could affect his business, but he would do just that if it became necessary to protect his mole in the DA's office.

CHAPTER TWENTY-THREE

Muriel smiled when she saw Naomi Baker unreel from her chair in the waiting room of the Multnomah district attorney's office. Naomi had played volleyball in college, and she was one of the few women attorneys who dwarfed Muriel.

Muriel and Naomi had taken the bar exam together and became friends. After she passed, Naomi went to work at a law firm that had a contract to handle court-appointed cases, and they had locked horns a few times when they were both handling misdemeanors. The cases had been hard fought, but the friends didn't let that stand in the way of a post-trial dinner after the verdict came in.

"What's up, Naomi?" Muriel asked.

"Billy Kramer. I'm his lawyer, and I was told that you have the case."

"I do. Come on back to my office."

"What are you going to charge Kramer with?" Naomi asked when they were seated with the door closed.

"That's a difficult question to answer. From what I know, the charges could be everywhere from theft to murder."

"Theft of Terrance Cogen's Jaguar?"

Muriel nodded.

"That might be tough to prove. Kramer was Cogen's chauffeur. He had every right to drive that car."

"He didn't have the right to gift it to Jack Blackburn."

"Who says it was a gift? Billy was too intoxicated to drive, so he asked Blackburn to drive his girlfriend home. He never intended Blackburn to keep the car. Cogen's address was on the registration. Blackburn could have returned the Jag, but he chose to steal it."

"Cynthia Woodruff will testify that Billy only pretended to be drunk when he gave Blackburn the keys to the Jag. She'll also testify that your client reported the car stolen so Blackburn would be charged with Cogen's murder."

"The testimony of an angry ex-girlfriend."

Muriel stared at her friend for a moment. Then she laughed. "What do you want, Naomi?"

Baker smiled. "Billy says he didn't kill Cogen. He was dead when he found the body, and he panicked."

"Why would he panic?"

"Here's where we start our negotiations, Muriel. Cogen was a crook. He scammed and embezzled a lot of money, and he washed it through legitimate businesses owned by really bad people. Billy could tell you all about the voyage that the money took."

"In exchange for . . . ?"

"The only thing you can get Kramer for involves the Jag, and you know what I'll argue, so winning even that case won't be a sure thing. Why don't you talk to your boss and see what she would be willing to do for insider information on the Lucifer's Disciples."

The mention of the biker gang unsettled Muriel. She didn't want anything to do with them, so she bought herself some time to think.

"I'll need a proffer and some reason to believe that Kramer didn't run away because he murdered Terrance Cogen."

"Let me talk to my client and get back to you. Meanwhile, what's your position on bail?"

"We can talk about bail after I see the proffer."

Normally, Muriel would have spent more time catching up on Naomi's work and social life, but she was anxious to be alone, so she made up a meeting she had to attend and sent Naomi on her way after the friends set a date to have lunch.

As soon as Naomi left, Muriel felt real fear. She had no idea that there was a connection between Terrance Cogen's case and the Disciples. Muriel was brave, but she wasn't foolhardy, and she had no desire to be in a situation that could cost her life. It was a little after four. She decided to go home while it was still light and try to figure out what she was going to do.

CHAPTER TWENTY-FOUR

Audrey Packer and Chad Remington were sitting at a table in a coffee shop when an elegantly dressed woman in her midfifties walked in. Dr. Valerie Girard was a psychiatrist who had testified for the State in a death penalty case Packer and Remington had investigated. Her silver-gray hair was cut short, her bright blue eyes sparkled like gems when she scanned the room, and she walked toward the detectives with the gait that she'd employed on the runway when she was a fashion model in her teens and early twenties, before she used the money she'd made to pay for medical school.

"Thanks for coming, Valerie," Chad said.

"How could I not after you told me that you wanted to ask my advice about an alien abduction?"

The detectives sat across from the psychiatrist, and Chad pushed the caffe latte he bought for her across the table.

"Is this my consulting fee?" Girard joked.

"If we deem your information worthwhile, there could be an almond croissant in your future."

"Yum. I'd perjure myself for an almond croissant."

"We'll settle for a rational explanation for a totally irrational one," Audrey said.

"I assume this concerns United States congressman Thomas Horan," the doctor said.

"You saw the interview?"

"I read about it. Then I found it on the internet, after you called."

"So, what do you think?"

"You mean, do I believe that he was poked and prodded by ETs in a flying saucer?"

Chad grinned. "No, Valerie. We both know that didn't happen. What I want is an explanation for his statements if we exclude the possibility that he's flat-out lying."

"I did a little research after you called, and I can give you a possible explanation for his behavior. But I need some more information. Do you know if the congressman had an experience that could have caused trauma shortly before he was found?"

"This is highly confidential. We think that Horan was at the scene of Terrance Cogen's murder. It was very gruesome, blood everywhere, and we know that he received a blow to the head from a blunt instrument. The blow was hard enough to cause a concussion."

"That's helpful, but anything I say is pure guesswork and not something I would swear to in court."

"Don't worry. This is just background."

"Okay. Well, I did some reading about alien abductions. Researchers at Harvard devised an experiment to determine if people who claim to have memories of being abducted by aliens would show the same psychological reactions shown by combat veterans, people who survive car accidents, and other people who have experienced similar traumatic experiences. They recruited six women and four men who claimed that they had been abducted by extraterrestrials. They were interviewed and also wrote a script that detailed their abduction. The research team made audiotapes that were spoken in a neutral voice from the scripts. While the subjects listened to the tapes, the researchers recorded their emotional responses using measures like their heart rate and sweat on the palms of their hands. The same procedure was used with eight people who were haunted by traumatic experiences that had nothing to do with being abducted by aliens. The results of the two groups were strikingly similar. The reactions for the alien abduction group were as great or greater than those of individuals who couldn't shake memories of combat, sexual abuse, or other traumatic events."

"How did the researchers explain these findings?" Chad asked. "I assume they didn't believe that the subjects had actually been abducted."

"No. They tried to explain the findings by referencing a phenomenon that's called *dreaming with your eyes open*."

"I think I've heard of that," Audrey said. "Isn't it called *sleep paralysis*?"

"Yes. The phenomenon happens when people awaken from a dream. When you dream, your body is paralyzed to prevent you from jumping out of bed or doing something else that might injure you. When the sleeper awakens before the paralysis goes away, they experience hallucinations like flashing lights or some kind of living thing lurking in the room. This experience can be frightening, and the dreamer may try to find meaning in it."

"Horan heard all sorts of tales of alien abductions during the congressional hearings," Chad said.

Valerie nodded.

"The congressman and his car were discovered in Silverton,

some distance from his home and the place where Cogen was killed," Audrey said. "He claims that he has no idea how he got there. Do you have an explanation for how that might have happened?"

"Yes, but again, this is just between us."

"That's understood."

"Okay, then. Have you ever heard of a dissociative fugue?"

"Can't say as I have," Chad said.

"I think it was discussed in my college psych course," Audrey said.

"What is it?" Chad asked.

"Memory loss is a defense mechanism to protect a person from recalling disturbing or painful events," Dr. Girard answered. "Dissociative fugue is a symptom where a person with memory loss travels or wanders. That leaves a person in an unfamiliar setting with no memory of how they got there. This usually happens with conditions caused by severe trauma."

"So, Horan could have driven to Silverton, ditched his car, and wandered into the farmer's field," Chad said.

"It's possible," Girard agreed.

"Will Horan recover his memory?" Chad asked.

"Fugue states can last for days or months."

"So, he should regain his memory, if he's not faking?" Audrey asked.

"He could, but I can't say how quickly that will happen."

"Is there anything you could do to speed up the process?"

Dr. Girard thought for a moment. Then she said, "There might be," and told the detectives her idea.

The detectives and the psychiatrist talked a little longer. Then Chad sent Dr. Girard on her way with a little white bag containing an almond croissant.

"So, Chad, do you think Horan was at the estate when Cogen was murdered?" Audrey asked.

Chad nodded. "If he didn't do the deed himself, he may have seen who did."

"I vote for the latter possibility. Someone bashed him in the head really hard."

"Our killer."

"Yeah. He walks in before the killer leaves. That would explain why he was attacked."

"If Valerie is right, he may be able to tell us whodunit when he recovers his memory."

"We still have a problem," Audrey said.

"Oh?"

"After that television interview, who would believe anything he said?"

Chad sighed. "You're right. What do you think we should do next?"

"I want to talk to Francine Horan. Then I think we should bring Frank Curtin up to date."

Thomas Horan had told Francine that he would have to hire a new PR person when they married because his opponent could use his employing his wife as ammunition in a campaign. Francine wasn't upset. Doing PR for Tom was exhausting, and she was grateful for the break. Then Tom had gone public with his claim that he had been abducted by aliens, and she was even more grateful that she didn't have to deal with the blowback.

Francine was getting ready to go to her Pilates class when the doorbell rang. She looked through the peephole and saw the two detectives who had been upsetting Tom. She debated pretending that she wasn't in, but curiosity got the better of her.

"He's in DC," Francine said.

"We know, Mrs. Horan. It's you we want to talk to," Chad said.

"About what?"

"We think we've found a rational explanation for Congressman Horan's alien abduction claim, and we know a way to help your husband. Can we come in?"

Tom's obsession with his alien abduction was making him sick. He had horrible nightmares when he slept, and he was depressed and frightened when he was awake. Francine wished there was some way she could help him, so she ushered the detectives into her living room.

"I know everybody thinks I broke up Tom's marriage and that I don't love him. But Tom wanted to get away from Millie, and I do love him. And I know he's been suffering. If you know a way I can help, please tell me."

Chad told Francine what he and Audrey had learned from Dr. Girard.

"We're pretty certain that your husband was in Terrance Cogen's living room around the time he was killed," Chad said. "We think the killer caused the concussion that led to his hallucinations about being abducted by aliens. We want you to convince your husband to let Dr. Girard hypnotize him. That may be the key to finding Terrance Cogen's killer and helping the congressman recover his memory."

"Hypnosis? I don't know."

"Would you be willing to meet with Dr. Girard so she can explain what she would be doing?"

"She really thinks she can help Tom?"

"She's not certain, but she thinks this might work."

"All right, I'll meet with her."

Frank Curtin was a baby-faced politician with a fabulous smile who had arrived at the position of Multnomah County district attorney by an unusual and circuitous route. Curtin was the only child of a wealthy Portland family. He'd gone undergraduate to an Ivy on the East Coast, but he had political ambitions, and he had come home for law school.

As soon as he passed the bar, Curtin had become a public defender who battled the occupants of the office he would eventually lead. After four years, he had left the public defender's office and won a spot in the state legislature. Two successful terms later, he threw his hat in the ring when the Multnomah County DA retired, running as a reform prosecutor who would stop prosecuting drug possession cases in favor of referrals to mental health facilities and wipe out corruption in the Portland Police Bureau. These positions had not won him many supporters in the police and the office he intended to run, but it had swayed the liberal voters who dominated Multnomah County politics. Thomas Horan had been one of his biggest supporters, and Curtin had made it clear to Packer and Remington that he wanted constant updates on Horan's case.

"So, where do we stand?" Curtin asked Remington and Packer after they told him what they'd learned from Valerie Girard.

"We're pretty certain that Congressman Horan was at the estate around the time Cogen was killed," Chad said.

"You don't think Tom murdered Cogen, do you?" Curtin asked.

"We're not leaning that way."

"Good, good. Tom is a dear friend and a staunch supporter. We were on the board of the Westmont, and he was involved in my first run for the legislature."

"We understand that," Chad assured Curtin. "We do think that he may have seen the murderer."

Curtin nodded. "The blow to the head. Though that may tell us that he didn't see the killer. If he had, Terrance's killer would most probably have killed Tom too, don't you think?"

"That's a good point," Chad said.

"You said that Dr. Girard thinks Tom may recover his memory soon. When he does, we'll know what happened. But tell me, do you think that Tom is in danger? Will the killer go after him?"

"He hasn't so far. He may think that no one will believe anything the congressman says after his claim of being abducted by aliens. And assassinating a US congressman would bring unbelievable heat down on him."

"Too true. Well, thanks for the update. Keep me posted if there are any new developments. You're doing great work."

The detectives left Curtin's office. Audrey waited to say what was on her mind until they were alone in the elevator. "That was interesting."

"How so?" Chad asked.

"Don't you find Curtin's interest in this case a bit unhealthy?"

"I don't know. He said Horan is an old friend and big supporter. It's natural that he'd be interested."

"I think he's a little too interested."

Chad frowned. "What are you suggesting?"

"Nothing I can put my finger on. I just get the feeling that Curtin has more than a professional interest in the Cogen case."

CHAPTER TWENTY-FIVE

Muriel and Naomi Baker were waiting in a contact visiting room at the jail when the guards led Billy Kramer in.

"Billy, this is Muriel Lujack," Naomi said. "She's the district attorney who is in charge of your case."

Kramer was a con man with movie star good looks, and Muriel expected him to turn on the charm. She wasn't disappointed.

Billy beamed a smile at Muriel while he was taking a seat.

"I'm glad to meet you, Miss Lujack," Billy said. "I hope we can work together."

"That depends on what you tell me," Muriel replied in a tone that was all business. "Miss Baker says that you have information about Terrance Cogen's murder and his fraudulent activities. I won't be able to tell you anything until I hear what you have to say. I will guarantee you that nothing you say at this conference will be used against you, so you can speak freely. You do need to know that I will prosecute you to the utmost of my ability if I find that you've lied or misled me. Miss Baker can tell you that I mean what I say."

Naomi took a document out of her attaché case that set out the agreement between the parties with respect to the proffer. Muriel, Kramer, and Baker signed the document.

"Let's get your version of what happened on the evening that Mr. Cogen was murdered," Muriel said.

"Right. That's really important. You need to know that I had nothing to do with Mr. Cogen getting killed."

"Okay."

"Sometime in the afternoon—I think it was around four or so—Mr. Cogen gave me a briefcase and told me to bring it to this business he had an investment in. So, I drove there and dropped off the briefcase."

"What is the name of the business?" Muriel asked.

"Why do you need to know that?"

"Your job during this interview is to answer my questions. If that's a problem, I can leave and ask a grand jury to indict you for murder."

"No, no, that's no problem," Kramer answered quickly. "I went to Cady's Garage and Auto Repair. It's on Eighty-Second."

"What was in the briefcase?"

"I didn't look."

Muriel stared at Kramer. "Make a guess. And remember that we aren't playing games."

Kramer's head bobbed up and down. "Yeah, I get that. So, if I had to guess, I'd say there was money in the briefcase."

"You may continue."

"After I dropped off the briefcase, I had a few beers and a burger at a bar with some of the guys at the garage. It was dark when I headed back. Where Cogen lives, there are a lot of country lanes and the lighting ain't that great. When I was almost back, a car went by me. It was going fast, and I didn't see the driver."

"Can you tell me the make of the car?"

"No. Like I said, it was dark and the car sped by. I'm not even sure it was coming from Cogen's estate, but I want to tell you everything."

"Go on."

"I got back to the house and went in to tell Mr. Cogen that I'd done what he sent me to do. And that's when I found him lying on the floor with blood all over the place."

"What did you do when you saw the body?" Muriel asked.

"I felt for a pulse to see if he was really dead. Then . . ." Kramer shook his head. "I'm not proud of what I did next. Especially what I did to Jack Blackburn. But I panicked, because I didn't want to get blamed for the murder."

"Go on."

"I got out of there as fast as I could. Cogen was involved in all kinds of bad shit. Not violent crimes. Embezzling, money scams. I helped him with some of it. I was afraid I'd be the number one suspect in his murder. Even if I wasn't, an investigation could get me in hot water if the cops found out that I was involved with his other schemes."

"Tell me about Jack Blackburn," Muriel said.

"Yeah, about Jack. I know this makes me sound like the worst person, but I was really scared. I remembered Jack saying how crazy he was about cars, and he knew all about them. I was sure he'd go nuts if I let him drive the Jag. I called Cynthia and told her to go to this bar near where Jack lives. Then I called Jack and told him to meet me there in an hour. Then I drove the Jag to a parking lot near the bar and waited for Jack to show up.

"The plan was that Cynthia would say she had to get home, and I'd say I was too drunk to drive her. Then we got Jack to drive the Jag, and I drove Cynthia's car to a prearranged place to meet her and get out of town. Soon after we were on our way, I reported the Jag stolen."

Kramer looked across the table. "I wouldn't have let him get convicted. I swear. I was gonna come back and clear Jack if it looked bad for him."

Muriel shot Kramer a look that told him that she didn't believe a word of what he'd just said.

"Let's move on from the murder. Cady's garage is owned by the Lucifer's Disciples, isn't it?"

"Mr. Cady runs the place, but some of the Disciples work there."

"Remember, you're supposed to be completely honest with me."

"I'm trying to be. I ain't seen the ownership papers, so I can't say for sure."

"Can you tell me, for sure, how many times you brought briefcases full of cash to the garage?"

"I done it a lot. I can't give you the exact number."

Muriel felt sick when she asked the next question, but she knew she had to do it.

"Why don't you tell me what you know about Mr. Cogen's business with the Disciples."

As soon as Muriel left the jail, she called Ellen Kaufman and told her she was on her way to tell her what she'd learned. Muriel was surprised and a little frightened when she saw Oscar Vanderlasky waiting with her boss. Ellen was on her list of suspects, but she wasn't high up. Oscar was the deputy she worried about the most.

"Do you believe him?" Ellen asked when Muriel finished a summary of her conversation with Kramer.

"About his involvement in the murder?"

Ellen nodded.

"He admitted to being at Cogen's place on the evening he was killed, and he framed Jack Blackburn for the killing, but I . . ." Muriel shook her head. "I'm up in the air about his guilt."

"Blackburn's our guy," Vanderlasky said confidently.

"What about the beer glass?" Ellen asked.

"What beer glass?" Muriel asked.

"Didn't you ask him about the beer glass?" Ellen asked.

"I don't know what you're talking about."

Ellen told Muriel about the glass with Blackburn's prints that had been found at the crime scene.

"I didn't know about the glass," Muriel said. "I just got the case, and I haven't had time to read all the reports in Cogen's murder."

"Do we know the glass came from the bar where Blackburn met Kramer?" Ellen asked Vanderlasky.

"The glass is like the ones they use at the bar. That doesn't mean Blackburn is innocent," Vanderlasky insisted. "It's a very common type. Cogen could have owned one."

"We'll have to give Wyatt a report of Kramer's statement," Ellen said. "It's exculpatory evidence."

Vanderlasky did not look happy.

"What should we do with Kramer?" Ellen asked.

"We can still stick him and Blackburn with the theft of the Jaguar," Vanderlasky said. "That will keep them in jail until we sort out the murder charge."

"I promised Kramer's lawyer that I wouldn't oppose bail if the proffer was useful," Muriel said.

Vanderlasky's cheeks turned scarlet. "What the fuck, Lujack? He's a flight risk. Did you forget that?"

"I don't think he'll run again," Muriel answered without much conviction. She didn't trust Kramer, but she had made a promise to Naomi, and she was honor bound to keep it.

"If she made a deal with Kramer's lawyer, she has to stick to it," Ellen said.

Then she turned to Muriel. "I wish you'd run that by me before you involved the office."

"I'm sorry, but Kramer wouldn't have talked otherwise."

Ellen sighed. "What's done is done."

Then she turned to Vanderlasky. "If you get the evidence you need to indict for murder, we can revoke the bail and get him back behind bars. So, get to work."

CHAPTER TWENTY-SIX

Valerie Girard walked into her waiting room when her receptionist told her that Francine Horan and the two detectives had arrived. The psychiatrist could see that Francine was very nervous, so she smiled in an attempt to put her at ease.

"Thanks for coming to see me, Mrs. Horan. I imagine that it hasn't been very pleasant for you since your husband disappeared."

"It's been a nightmare."

"I hope I can help him."

"How exactly are you planning to do that?"

Valerie looked at Remington and Packer. "I hope you don't mind, but I'd like you to wait out here while I talk to Mrs. Horan. Is that okay?"

"That's fine," Audrey said.

"Then why don't you come back to my office," Valerie said.

When they were seated on a sofa in the doctor's office, Valerie asked Francine if she wanted a cup of coffee or tea.

"No, thank you. What I do want is to learn how you think you can help Tom. The detectives said that you want to hypnotize him."

"I do."

"All I know about hypnotism is what I've seen on TV shows. Can you explain what you want to do and why it will help?"

Valerie could see that Francine was tense, and she thought of a way to relax her.

"You know, the way hypnosis was discovered as a tool for helping people is a strange tale. Franz Anton Mesmer was a Viennese physician who believed that the planets influenced the human body. In 1776, he wrote a paper stating that this action occurred through the instrumentality of a universal fluid in which all bodies were immersed. He believed that the fluid, which was invisible, could be withdrawn by the human will from one point and concentrated in another. Mesmer theorized that an inharmonious distribution of these fluids throughout the body produced disease. Health could be attained by establishing harmony of the magnetic fluids. Mesmer believed that a force, which he called *animal magnetism*, emanated from his hands directly into the patient, thereby enabling him to adjust the internal imbalances in the fluids and eradicate disease in the patient.

"Unfortunately for Mesmer, he effected a startling and rapid cure in a young girl suffering from an imposing array of physical symptoms through the use of magnets the first time he put his theory into practice. This led him to spend his career trying to convince the medical community of the soundness of his theory.

"The Vienna medical fraternity thought Mesmer was a fraud, and he was forced to flee to Paris. In 1781, he founded a clinic there. Mesmerism became a fad among the wealthy, but he was discredited by a commission appointed by the French government, and he retired to Switzerland.

"However, mesmerism did lead to an interesting discovery. The Marquis de Puységur noticed that mesmerized subjects could hear only what the magnetizer said and were oblivious to everything else. They accepted suggestions without question and could recall nothing of the events of the trance when restored to consciousness. Puységur called this condition *artificial somnambulism* and explained that a subject in this state could accomplish amazing feats like reading sealed messages, suffering needles to be jabbed into their skin, and permitting without flinching the application of a red-hot poker to their bodies."

Valerie smiled. "Don't worry. I'm not going to stick pins in your husband or jab him with a red-hot poker, but I am going to use hypnosis to put him in a state where he is open to suggestion. Then I'll try to get him to remember the incident that caused his trauma."

"How do you do that?"

"Good question. I just suggested that you have a cup of coffee. You weighed the suggestion and turned me down. However, if I suggest that everything I am going to suggest is reasonable, and you accept that suggestion, you will stop evaluating, and you will depend on me."

Valerie placed a piece of paper on the coffee table and placed a dot on the top of the page.

"Think of this point as a state of complete alertness. You are alert now. You can see and hear everything that is going on in my office. You can listen to our conversation and think your own thoughts. But there are other states of awareness that are not total."

Valerie drew a straight line down the paper and ended it with another dot.

"You know the expression *dead to the world*? A person is so sound asleep that their mind is almost totally at rest. That's what this dot represents.

"Along this line, we're going to get various stages of alertness. Somewhere on the line is a point where a person is in a state where he is susceptible to suggestion. This might be at a point where a person has been in bed for thirty minutes. His eyes are closed, he's lost contact with the general sounds around him, but he's still aware of important sounds, like a baby crying. If you ask a person in this state a question, the answer will be accurate.

"If a person has been in a situation that was so frightening that they have repressed the memory of the event to the point where they deny they were even there, I may be able to use hypnosis to get them to talk about the event, to relive it by developing a hypnotic state to relax the individual. When the person is relaxed, the repressive mechanisms that watch over the frightening memories are off guard. The relaxation allows the repressed memories to be brought from the subconscious to the conscious. But it's not an easy process, especially when you're dealing with amnesia that's due to a terrifying experience."

"If I can convince Tom to see you, will you try to help him?" Francine asked.

"I would like the chance."

PART FOUR

DEAD ENDS

CHAPTER TWENTY-SEVEN

Billy Kramer thanked Naomi Baker as soon as the judge set his bail. Then he asked her if she wanted to celebrate with him. Kramer thought Baker was hot and he was disappointed when she turned him down, but his good mood returned as soon as he was out of jail.

Billy's first problem was finding a place to live. He couldn't go back to his apartment over the garage, for obvious reasons, and bunking with Cynthia was out. He'd asked and she told him that she'd been kicked out of her apartment and didn't ever want to see him again. Fortunately, Billy had money. He'd pleaded poverty to get a court-appointed lawyer, but he'd been skimming a little off the top of the cash he'd helped Terrance Cogen launder long enough to have amassed a nice nest egg.

Cogen had made it clear that he didn't want Billy bringing

women to his apartment over the garage after one of his pickups caused a loud, drunken scene at the same time Terrance was hosting a dinner party, so Billy had gotten friendly with the owner of a motel the Disciples owned. That's where Billy partied, and it was where he paid for a room after getting out of jail, one of the dumbest things Billy had done during a lifetime of making poor decisions. Walter Zegda had put out the word that he was eager to get in touch with Billy, and the clerk called the Disciples' clubhouse as soon as Billy finished checking in.

After Billy took a nap, he'd gone to a tavern where he'd hit on a few women. He hadn't gotten lucky, but he had gotten very drunk. When he returned to his motel, Billy staggered into his room and flopped onto his bed without turning on the light. After a while, the urge to piss forced him to struggle to a sitting position. He gathered his strength and shuffled toward the bathroom. He was halfway there when he realized that someone was sitting in the dark in a corner of his room.

"What the fuck!" Billy screamed as he jumped backward. The edge of the bed caught Billy behind his knees, and he tumbled onto the covers, adrenaline bringing him to the edge of sobriety.

There was a lamp next to the armchair where the man was sitting. The light came on and illuminated Wolf Larson, who uncoiled from his chair in a way that reminded Billy of the scene in *Godzilla* where the monster rises up from the ocean to lay waste to Tokyo.

"Rough night, Billy?" Wolf asked.

Billy struggled to a sitting position and forced a smile so his visitor wouldn't see how terrified he was.

"It's great seeing you, Wolf."

"Same here. Glad you're out and about."

"I'd love to have a chat, but I'm pretty wasted, and I need my beauty sleep. Can we get together tomorrow?"

"Getting your forty winks will have to wait. Walt wants to congratulate you on your release from the pokey."

"Can't he do that tomorrow?"

"I'm afraid not. I have a chariot waiting below for a short trip across town. But I'm certain Walt will be considerate once he sees the shape you're in. The faster we go, the sooner you'll be in dreamland."

Terror helped Billy sober up during the trip to the garage Walter Zegda used as a torture chamber, and he was wide awake by the time he walked into the cavernous space.

Zegda crossed to the door and enveloped Billy in a hug.

"I'm so glad you're back in the world, Billy. As we both know, jail is not a happy place."

"No, it's not."

Walter had set up two chairs across from each other near the rear wall of the garage. Billy noticed that there was a large plastic sheet covering the space under and around his chair.

"Have a seat," Walt said.

Billy sat down, and Wolf walked behind him. Billy turned and looked at Larson. Wolf smiled.

"Hey, Billy, look at me," Zegda said.

Billy turned. He felt like he might throw up.

"Wolf called ahead and said you're a little under the weather. Do you need a pharmaceutical to help you sober up?"

"That's okay, Walt. I'm fine."

"Good, because I want you sharp so you can clear up what I am sure is a misunderstanding."

"What is?" Billy asked.

"Were you talking to deputy district attorney Muriel Lujack? Is my information correct?"

Billy started to sweat. "Well, yeah, Walt. You know how plea negotiations work. My lawyer was with me, and we listened to her offer."

"My information is that you did more than that."

"Oh. What did you hear?"

"Why don't you tell me what you said, and I'll see if it matches what I was told."

"You got nothing to worry about, Walt. The DA just wanted to know about Cogen. I didn't kill him, but I found his body. That's why I split. I thought they'd try to pin his murder on me."

"It seems they haven't, because you can't get bail in a murder case without a hearing, and you're out and about."

"Yeah. They admitted that they don't think I killed Terrance."

"Could there be another reason the authorities are treating you so well?"

"What do you mean?"

"Did you discuss Disciples business with Miss Lujack?"

"Hey, no. I'd never do that."

"Not even to fend off a charge of murder and get out of jail?"

"Hey, Walt, you and I go way back. We were on the football and wrestling teams in high school. We're pals. I wouldn't do anything to hurt you. You know that. You know me."

"I do, Billy. That's the problem. I know that with you, Billy always comes first."

Zegda looked over Billy's shoulder. "My oldest and dearest friend seems to be fidgeting, Wolf. Can you help him stay in one spot?"

Wolf stunned Billy with a blackjack. Then he secured his body to the chair. By the time he was through, Billy was starting to revive.

"How are you doing, Billy?" Zegda asked.

"Jeez, that hurts," Billy managed. "Why did you hit me?"

"You weren't truthful. Lying has consequences. Wolf is going to torture you now so we can learn everything you told the authorities."

Three-quarters of an hour later, Zegda was satisfied that he knew everything Kramer had told Muriel Lujack.

"That's enough, Wolf," Zegda said.

Wolf had worked up a sweat, and he swigged some water from a plastic bottle. Billy's eyes were glazed over, and his chin rested on his chest, which was covered in blood and saliva.

"Give our friend some water. I want him alert," Zegda said.

After a while, Billy was able to focus. Zegda took out his Rubik's Cube, and Wolf got out his stopwatch.

"Hey, Billy," Walt said. "I need you to focus, because you might just see history being made."

CHAPTER TWENTY-EIGHT

When Thomas Horan flew back to Washington, DC, after the UFO hearing, he was surrounded by reporters when he deplaned. When he went on TV and told his tale of being abducted by ETs, he was front-page news again. Then a sex scandal drew the members of the Fourth Estate toward new prey, and his tale of his abduction by aliens became old news. Horan couldn't figure out how to generate new interest in his campaign until Margo Sparks came to his office.

The ex–CIA agent was dressed in a cream-colored blouse, a severe gray skirt and jacket set, and her gray hair was cut tight to her face. She wore very little makeup and was all business once she, the congressman, and Eric Gilmore were seated in Horan's office.

Gilmore was a veteran of the political wars and had signed on as Horan's administrative assistant after managing his successful congressional bid. He was in his midforties and overweight, and his features were starting to show the first signs displayed by people who smoked and drank too much.

"It's good seeing you again," Horan told his guest. "I hope you have no ill feelings about the way I cross-examined you at the hearing."

Sparks smiled. "I expected to get worked over. Convincing anyone that aliens have visited Earth is a hard sell."

"I'm glad you've forgiven me for being overbearing at the hearing. So, why are we meeting?"

"That should be obvious. You are the most prominent person who has ever claimed to have seen extraterrestrials in person and to have visited an alien spacecraft. We can use your help to alert the American public to the cover-up that has been going on for so many years."

"The congressman is already the target of attacks on his credibility," Gilmore said. "Everything has quieted down in the past two weeks. I don't think it would be wise to stir things up again."

"Let's not be hasty, Eric," Horan said. He did not dread the publicity he'd received since he'd told his tale on *Wake Up, Portland*. The stories in the newspapers, TV, and radio were publicity his campaign did not have to pay for. Since the attention he received had tailed off, his main concern was how to get it up and running again, because, much to the surprise of his advisers, his polling numbers had gone up since he'd announced that he was the victim of an alien abduction.

"What did you have in mind for me to do?"

"Discover the Truth, our nonprofit, is holding a convention in two weeks. We would be honored to have you as our keynote speaker. The only thing we would want you to do is tell your story, which you've already done several times."

"I don't think that's wise, Tom," Gilmore said. "No offense, Mrs. Sparks. I know that you mean well, but there are a lot of crackpots in your organization, and I don't think it will help the congressman to be associated with them."

"I understand your position, Eric," Horan said, "but I'd like to think about Mrs. Sparks's offer. And now, I'm afraid I have to get to a committee meeting. It's been good seeing you again."

Horan worked on several pieces of legislation before meeting a lobbyist for dinner. He got back to his DC apartment a little after nine and watched a basketball game while he nursed a scotch. By the time the game ended, Horan was beat, and he had no trouble falling into a deep and troubled sleep.

When his dream began, the congressman found himself in a dark space where the only illumination was provided by the pale rays of moonlight that filtered through the gauzelike drapes that covered a French window. In the dream, he was having trouble breathing, and he crumpled to the floor. A thing loomed over him. It was ghostly white and shapeless. It leaned down, but his vision was blurry, and he couldn't make it out. Then he started to scream.

Moments later, Thomas Horan struggled up from his sweat-soaked sheets, his heart racing and his eyes wide open. The dream had been so real. The thing in it must have been one of his alien abductors, but was it? He concentrated, trying to bring back the image that had terrified him, but it was no use.

Horan got out of bed and walked into his kitchen. As he filled a glass with cold water, he thought about the nightmares that had haunted his sleep since he'd been found on the road next to the farmer's field. They were similar, but they were different. Lately, the thing he was seeing was growing more distinct. Was the thing a figment of his imagination, or was it real?

Almost nobody believed he'd been kidnapped by extraterrestrials. Psychiatrists who had been interviewed about his allegations called them false memories created in response to trauma. Were the memories false? When he dreamed, was his subconscious trying to make him remember what caused the trauma? He had been struck hard enough to cause a concussion. Was the blow delivered by an alien, or was there another explanation?

When he was calmer, Horan went back to bed. It took him a while before he succumbed to sleep. When he woke up, he felt ragged. After he washed up, he checked his phone. Francine had sent a text that said he should call her because she had something important that she wanted to discuss.

"Hi, honey," Horan said when his wife answered. "I got your text."

"I'm very worried about you."

"I know. It's the alien thing, right?"

"And your nightmares, and . . . You've been so depressed."

"Don't worry. I'm dealing with it."

"Those detectives visited me. They told me they know someone who can help you. It's a doctor, Valerie Girard. I talked to her. She thinks you suffered a terrible experience and that you're suppressing your memories of what happened. She told me that she might be able to help you, if you let her hypnotize you."

"I'm not seeing a shrink. If that got out, it would kill my chances to get elected."

"No one would have to know. You could fly back, and we could sneak you into her office."

There was dead air. Francine could hear Tom breathing.

"Please, Tom. I hate seeing you this way. Do it for me."

"I . . . I'll think about it."

"I love you. I want this to end."

"I love you too."

The call ended, and Horan put down his phone. He'd gone

through hell since he was abducted, and he hated that Francine was so worried. But hypnosis and seeing a shrink . . . He wanted the nightmares to end, but the publicity could destroy him. Still, if there was a chance that he could find out what really happened to him . . .

CHAPTER TWENTY-NINE

Gloria Pascal got together with her friends every weekend so they could ride their bikes on country roads. Along the way, they stopped for lunch and traded stories about work and family. Today's ride was on a mountain bike trail that was a challenge. But Gloria relished the challenge as much as she treasured these weekly adventures with her friends.

The trail they were following led through forest, and the shade was a relief from the heat. Gloria was feeling good and pedaling hard when her front wheel hit a concealed root and she tumbled sideways down a short incline.

The fall knocked the wind out of her, and she lay on her back, stunned, while her friends stopped and made their way to her.

"Are you okay?" Heidi Rich asked her.

Gloria sat up. "I don't think I broke anything."

"Can you stand up?" Megan Faraday asked.

Gloria struggled to her feet.

"Your bike looks okay," Heidi said.

"You're lucky. I crashed like this once and I—"

Heidi stopped midsentence. "Is that a person?" she asked, pointing to something wedged against a tree trunk at the bottom of the hill.

"I'm going to see that in my dreams tonight," Chad Remington said as he stared at Billy Kramer's mutilated body.

"This is really inconvenient," Oscar Vanderlasky complained.

"I bet it fucked up Kramer's plans too, Oscar," Audrey Packer replied, appalled by Vanderlasky's lack of empathy, but not surprised.

"Hey, the guy was a scumbag, but he was going to help me do some real damage to the Lucifer's Disciples. So, pardon me if I don't get all weepy."

Chad shook his head as the detectives began the climb to the top of the hill through the crowd of forensics experts who were combing the area for clues.

"Do you think Vanderlasky has human DNA?" Audrey asked.

"Don't ask me to bet on that," her partner answered.

"Do you think Walter Zegda did Billy in?"

"That's a bet I might take, if someone leaked what he told Muriel Lujack."

"Cogen's killer could have silenced him if he thought Kramer could out him."

"Zegda could have killed Cogen and Kramer."

"That's true. Kramer said Cogen and the Disciples were in business together. Cogen was facing a slew of criminal charges.

If Zegda was worried that Cogen would sell him out to make a deal, he wouldn't hesitate to kill him."

"I'm getting a headache," Audrey said.

"Sometimes I wish it were like TV, where every case gets wrapped up in an hour," Chad said with a shake of his head.

Jack Blackburn's trial was scheduled to begin soon, and Karen was worried. Oscar Vanderlasky's case rested on the evidence of the beer glass. Karen had asked Naomi Baker if she could ask her client about the glass, but Baker had refused to set up an interview until she had worked out a plea bargain.

Karen was working on a set of jury instructions in Blackburn's case when Morris Johnson walked into her office.

"I have good news and bad news," Johnson said after he shut the door to Karen's office and plopped down on one of her client chairs. "Which do you want first?"

"Hit me with the bad stuff so we can end on a high note."

"Billy Kramer is dead, and he didn't die easy. My sources are telling me that the kill looks like several murders attributed to Walter Zegda and the Lucifer's Disciples."

"Oh no," Karen Wyatt said. "There goes our chance to prove that Kramer brought the beer glass to Cogen's house."

"Did Cynthia Woodruff know he did?"

"I don't know. But anything she would try to tell a jury about what Kramer told her would be objected to as hearsay."

"Isn't there an exception to the hearsay rule that would let us get in what Kramer told her?"

Karen thought for a moment. Then she sat up and smiled. "There is."

Karen told Morris what she could argue if Oscar Vanderlasky tried to exclude statements Billy Kramer had made to Cynthia Woodruff or the police or DAs.

"You think that will work?" Morris asked.

"I'm pretty certain, but we don't even know if Kramer said anything to Woodruff or the authorities about the beer glass."

"I'll try to interview her, and I'll go through the discovery."

"Is that all the bad news?"

"It is."

"Then tell me something good."

"I went through the court records and found all the cases Muriel Lujack is handling. One of the defendants she's prosecuting is Raymond Castor. He's a Disciple, and one of the police reports lists Nikki Randolph as his girlfriend."

"You think that she's the person who told Muriel that her boyfriend knows the name of the DA on the take?"

"It has to be."

"What's your plan?"

"Money talks, bullshit walks."

"A charming phrase."

"But oh so true. DAs can't bribe people. We can."

CHAPTER THIRTY

Morris Johnson followed Nikki Randolph home. Her small Cape Cod was in a section of town where drug deals and gun violence were common. Many of the homes needed repair and were surrounded by unmown lawns dominated by weeds. Randolph's home was not one of them. It had a fresh coat of paint, a neat lawn, and a flower garden.

The Harley Nikki had ridden home from work was standing unprotected at the side of the house. Morris guessed that the neighborhood hoodlums saw enough Lucifer's Disciples at the house to know that theft of the hog would be punished by a slow death.

Morris opened the gate in the chain-link fence that surrounded the property, walked up the slate path, and rang the doorbell. Moments later, Nikki Randolph was standing in the doorway.

"Miss Randolph?" Morris inquired.

Randolph looked puzzled and a little worried. Morris guessed that the only men in suits who came to houses in her neighborhood were Jehovah's Witnesses or cops.

"My name is Morris Johnson, and I'd like to offer you a large sum of money."

Randolph scowled. "If you're selling something, I'm not interested."

"I'm an investigator for Karen Wyatt. I think you know who she is."

"The lawyer who went to prison."

Morris nodded. "I want to tell you about an interesting offer she wants to make you. But we're attracting attention from your neighbors."

Nikki peered over Johnson's shoulder and saw several people watching them.

"Can I come in and tell you why I'm here?"

Nikki hesitated. Then she stepped aside and ushered Morris into her living room.

"What's this about?" Nikki asked when they were seated.

"We know Ray-Ray knows the name of the Multnomah County DA who is working with the Disciples. Miss Wyatt believes that this person is part of the conspiracy that framed her. We want that name, and Miss Wyatt is willing to pay a lot of money to get it. She'll also try to get Ray a deal that will keep him out of prison."

Randolph looked stunned. "Did Lujack talk to you?"

"Miss Lujack did not give us your name, and it doesn't matter how I figured out that I had to talk to you. Get me the name and you get a substantial amount of money."

"Which Ray-Ray and me won't be able to spend if we're dead."

"Miss Randolph, I was a detective for many years, so you don't have to tell me about Walter Zegda."

"Then you know what happens to people who cross him."

"Miss Wyatt has been trying to find the people who framed her ever since she got out of prison. Getting that name is the central point in her life. No one needs to know who gave the name to us. And she will pay you and Ray enough to let you go anywhere you feel you will be safe. As an added bonus, once we have the name, we can use the DA to nail Zegda and eliminate the threat he might pose to you."

Morris let Randolph think. After a while, she looked at him.

"How much money are you offering?"

"I'm going to give you a figure. There won't be any bargaining. We're firm on that. So, if Ray or you try to bargain it up, it won't work. Understood?"

Nikki nodded.

"Three million dollars."

Nikki's eyes went wide, and Morris heard the intake of her breath.

"We can have a financial adviser invest it for you so it can grow, if you are interested. Or we will deposit it anywhere you want."

"All I have to do is get Ray-Ray to give me a name?"

"That's it. Of course, we'll check out the person to make sure Ray's info is the real deal."

"I get that."

"Do you need some time to think?"

"I need to talk to Ray-Ray."

Morris stood up and handed Nikki his card. "That's my cell. You can get me anytime. Let me know when you and Ray have made a decision."

As soon as the door closed behind the investigator, Nikki

Randolph poured herself a stiff drink. She had grown up in a trailer park without a father. Her mother worked as a bartender at a tavern patronized by the Disciples. That's how she'd met Ray-Ray.

Nikki hated living in the trailer park, and she'd made sure to graduate high school so she could get a job that would pay enough so she could move into a place of her own. Through hard work and study, she had gotten a job with a decent salary, and there were benefits like health insurance. She had a savings account with five hundred dollars in it. It had taken her a few years to accumulate that much, what with payments for the mortgage and expenses, but she was realistic enough to know that she lived paycheck to paycheck. Three million dollars was an unbelievable amount of money. She couldn't even imagine what it would be like to have that much cash. The problem was that they would have to betray Walter Zegda and the Disciples to earn it.

Nikki thought she would be willing to take the risk. She was terrified of Zegda, but she dreaded the thought of losing Ray-Ray to a long prison term. The big problem was Ray-Ray. He was a true believer in the biker life, and she wasn't sure how he would react. The only way she could find out was to talk to him.

CHAPTER THIRTY-ONE

Raymond Castor didn't have any problem spending time in jail, where he was an apex predator. Of course, he liked beer and pussy, which were unavailable in the pokey, but his lawyer was optimistic about his legal prospects, so he wasn't too worried about how long he would have to go without his Harley, Coors, and women.

Ray was reading a graphic novel in his cell when the guard announced that he had a visitor. He wasn't surprised when the guard led him into the narrow concrete cubicle that was used for noncontact visits and saw Nikki Randolph on the other side of the bulletproof glass. He knew that she had the hots for him. What did surprise him was how nervous she looked.

There were receivers attached to the wall on either side of the glass. Ray picked his up.

"Hey, babe. Nice of you to visit. Do you miss me?"

"You know I do."

"My lawyer thinks we'll beat the case, so I'll be out of here soon."

"I don't know if your lawyer is right," Nikki said as she tried to build up the courage to tell Ray the reason she was at the jail.

"Oh? Do you know something?"

Nikki's mouth was dry, and she wished she could get a drink of water, but she couldn't and she decided to take the plunge.

"I . . . I talked with Miss Lujack, the DA who has your case."

Ray did not look happy. "Why would you do that?"

Nikki looked down. "I wanted to help you. I told her you were innocent."

"Did you do anything else?"

"That's why I'm here. Something weird happened. It could make all the difference for us."

"Tell me about this weird thing, Nikki."

Nikki lowered her voice and whispered, "We can have a lot of money, Ray. Enough to set us up for life. Enough so we can go anywhere we want and live like rich people."

"I'm listening."

"Okay. So, I tried to make a deal with Lujack. I said you knew the name of a DA who was helping the Disciples."

Ray's face turned scarlet with rage, and he leaned forward until it was inches from the glass.

"You did what?!"

"Don't get mad, Ray-Ray. Listen to what happened."

"This better be fucking good."

"It is. I promise. This guy showed up at my house. He's an investigator for Karen Wyatt, the lawyer who was framed and went to prison. He said Wyatt would pay a lot of money for the name of the person who helped frame her. A lot of money!"

"How much, Nikki?"

"Three million dollars," she whispered.

Ray didn't blink. If he was shocked by the number, he didn't show it.

"All I have to do for the money is give Wyatt the name?" Ray asked.

"That's what he said."

"Walt has guys in here who would off me for a pack of cigarettes. I wouldn't last a minute in here if I outed the DA."

"The investigator said that Wyatt would help you get out of jail. She must have got the info from Lujack, so she'd know Lujack was going to help you if you helped her. As soon as the DA is arrested, she'll cut a deal that will destroy the Disciples.

"We'll be long gone, Ray-Ray. We can live like royalty with three million dollars. We can go to an island, somewhere Walter can't find us."

"You heard what happened to Billy Kramer? He thought he could hide from Walt. My lawyer said they're still hunting for some of his body parts."

Nikki leaned forward. "Kramer didn't have three million dollars, and we can get witness protection or help changing our names."

"You shouldn't have told Lujack about the Disciples' business."

"I did it for you, Ray. I did it for us."

Ray stopped looking through the glass. Nikki could see he was upset.

"I gotta think," he said after a while.

"Sure, Ray-Ray. I get it. It's a big decision. But try to make up your mind. I don't know how much longer Wyatt will stay with the offer."

Ray looked at Nikki. "I get that, babe. I won't keep you waiting."

"I love you, Ray."

Ray smiled. "I love you too."

Ray's smile disappeared as soon as Nikki was out of sight.

He couldn't believe that the idiot had gone to the DA. What she'd done could get both of them killed.

Ray knew why she'd done it. Nikki had a crush on him. That made it easy to get her into bed. She wasn't half-bad, but that was all. He had never been—what did they call it—monogamous. He liked to spread his love around. When Nikki had asked him to move in with her, he'd made up a bullshit story about why he had to keep his pad for Disciples business. He couldn't even remember what he'd told her. Running away with Nikki and having to spend the rest of his life with her as a ball and chain was not ever going to happen. Still, three million dollars was tempting. Except that he would have to give up the outlaw life, and Ray loved being a renegade with its constant adrenaline rush.

An hour after Ray was back in his cell, he made a decision and told the guard he wanted to talk to his lawyer.

CHAPTER THIRTY-TWO

Walter Zegda didn't do jails or prisons. He assumed anything he said would be recorded and used against him. So, he had Frank Tyler, a coke-addicted lawyer, on a retainer, which was paid in part in cash and in larger part in white powder. Anything anyone said to Tyler would be protected by the attorney-client privilege and couldn't be used to screw Zegda.

Raymond Castor was represented by Tyler, who had no qualms about repeating any of his "confidential" conversations with any of his clients to Zegda that the lawyer thought his master might need to know.

Half an hour after Ray called him, he and Tyler were conferring in a contact visiting room. The lawyer and his client leaned across the table until their heads were almost touching. Ray told Tyler what Nikki had told him in a voice barely above a whisper because he was as paranoid as Zegda about the ability of the authorities to record jailhouse conversations.

"What do you want me to do?" Tyler asked.

"You got to tell you-know-who. Wyatt is on the warpath. If she gets to the DA, the Disciples are fucked."

"You're right. I have to tell him," Tyler said, as careful as Ray not to name names.

"But tell him to go easy on Nikki. She doesn't know anything. I never told her the DA's name. She's got the hots for me, and she was just trying to help me."

Tyler nodded. "I'll do that. And you're doing the right thing, Ray."

Walter Zegda lived in an ultramodern, cantilevered glass-and-steel house that extended out over thick woods on one of the hills on Portland's west side. Wolf Larson thought his friend sounded nervous when he summoned him to his retreat in the middle of the night.

Zegda had his house swept for bugs every day, but he was still paranoid, so Wolf found him outside his house on a wide deck that gave Zegda a spectacular view of the lights of Portland at night and the snowcapped mountains of the Cascade Range when the sun was up.

"What's up?" Larson asked.

"I have a decision to make, and I want your input," Zegda said after he told Larson what Frank Tyler had told him.

"You're not thinking about taking out Wyatt."

"It would solve the problem."

"Hey, man. It's one thing to take care of a nobody like Kramer, but you'll bring down too much heat if you go after a prominent attorney. And how did Ray learn what he knows?"

"Yeah, that was my fault. I let it slip one night when Ray-Ray and I were drinking. I was stupid, but what's done is done. Ray-Ray knows the name, and three million dollars is one big incentive to share it with Wyatt."

"Wyatt isn't the problem," Larson said. "She doesn't have the name. If Raymond never tells her, she never will."

"You think I should take out Ray-Ray?"

Larson shrugged. "Once he's out of the picture, the problem is solved."

CHAPTER THIRTY-THREE

Raymond Castor was trying to nap when his cell door opened.

"Get your shit together, Castor. You're getting out."

Castor was groggy, and he wasn't sure he'd heard the guard correctly. "I'm getting out?"

"That's what I said. Someone posted your bail."

"Who?"

"I got no idea. Chop, chop. I got things to do."

Ray signed his discharge papers and was sent down to the waiting area. Karen Wyatt and Morris Johnson stood up when Ray walked out of the jail elevator.

"Mr. Castor, I'm Karen Wyatt, and I posted your bail."

All the color drained from Ray's face. "You just signed my death warrant, lady."

"Or I made you a rich man with the means to disappear. I

assume Miss Randolph told you about the three million dollars when she visited you in jail."

"How did you know she visited me?"

"I'm a very rich woman, Mr. Castor. Money buys information. It also buys freedom. Give me the name of the prosecutor who helped set me up, and I'll fly you anywhere you want to go on a private jet. We're talking a new identity and a fresh start. All in exchange for a name."

Ray's head swiveled as he looked to see who was listening. "I gotta go!"

He sounded panicky.

Karen stuck one of her cards in his shirt pocket.

"I can fix this. I can get the DA to drop your case."

"Can you stop me from being dead? Because you just killed me if anyone learns that you posted my bail and talked to me," Ray said. Then he pushed past Karen and hurried out to the street.

Karen Wyatt wasn't the only one who paid for information about the goings-on at the Multnomah County jail and courthouse. As soon as Walter Zegda learned that Karen Wyatt had posted Raymond Castor's bail, he sent Gabby Wright to spy on Castor.

"Wyatt was waiting for Ray-Ray, and they parleyed," Wright said into his phone.

"Could you hear what they said?"

"No. I couldn't get close enough. But Ray-Ray ran away like he was scared to death."

"Okay, Gabby. Stay on him. I want to know where he goes."

CHAPTER THIRTY-FOUR

Raymond Castor's D average in high school was the result of grade inflation. None of his teachers wanted to flunk him, because that would mean he would be left back, and they were as anxious as he was to get him out of their high school.

There was one test on which he received an A-plus. It was the test in citizen's education about the Second Amendment to the United States Constitution, which contained information about the right to bear arms. Ray loved guns almost as much as he loved his Harley.

He enlisted as soon as he was free of his mandatory sentence to high school. He didn't love the discipline in the army, but he loved being able to shoot guns. When he was shipped overseas to a combat zone, it was like dying and going to heaven. After shooting targets his whole life, he finally got a chance to shoot people.

Unfortunately, his problem with discipline caused him to be cast out of heaven when he was brought up on charges for striking a superior officer. When he got back to the States, he was despondent, but his spirits lifted when he ran into an old friend from high school who was running with the Lucifer's Disciples and knew how Ray could continue to get all kinds of guns.

Ray rented a house in the country. It was small and run-down, but it had a big backyard where he could shoot his guns to his heart's content. As soon as he was home, he loaded his arsenal, set booby traps around the house, and turned off all the lights to make it look like he was asleep. Maybe Walt didn't know about the three million dollars, but Ray was certain he would know that he was out on bail that Karen Wyatt had posted. Ray was not one of the Disciples' inner circle. He was a foot soldier. That made him expendable.

There was a shed where he kept his mower and other gardening equipment. It had holes in the walls that gave him a view of the front and back of his property. The Disciples dealt a lot of meth, so Ray wasn't the least bit tired when the killers came a little after three in the morning, which is the time when people were usually in a deep sleep.

There were four men. They came through the woods behind the house. Ray didn't recognize any of them, which meant that Walt had brought in a hit squad. The men scattered. Two moved toward the front door, and two went to the door that led into the kitchen. Ray eased out of the shed. He was wearing black and had blackened his face. He heard a scream from the kitchen. One of the booby traps had worked. It drew the attention of the men at the front door away from the shed. He fired, and one of the assassins pitched forward. The other man spun toward him, and Ray shot him in the chest. If only one of the men near the kitchen was dead or incapacitated, that left one man to deal with.

The quarter moon produced very little light, and the thick foliage in the trees in the side yard blocked some of that light. Ray edged around the side of the house until he could see the kitchen door. It was wide open, and he saw flames in the kitchen. He crouched and duckwalked toward the door. He was about to peek in when a branch snapped.

The last assassin had jumped away from the house when the booby trap exploded, and he had taken cover behind one of the trees in the side yard, figuring correctly that Ray would come to see how many men the booby trap had killed.

Ray dropped to the ground. Bullets sailed over the space his body had just occupied and embedded themselves in the wall of the house. Ray was flat on his back. He fired several times to chase the killer away. Then he raced around the front of the house to shield himself.

"It ain't worth it," Ray called out. "You stay here and there's a good chance you'll end up as dead as your buddies. Call this a draw and take off. I got no beef with you."

Ray waited for an answer. When none came, he took out a grenade and threw it toward the tree his assailant was using for cover. The blast shook the tree, and Ray heard a grunt of pain.

"Okay!" a man shouted moments later. "I'm going!"

"Take off. I promise I won't try to kill you."

Moments later, Ray saw a man hobbling toward the woods. He had lied about not trying to kill the last assassin. He fired at him, but he missed. The killer ran a zigzag path. Ray fired again, but the man made it to the trees. Ray thought about hunting him down, but the woods would provide cover that could be used for an ambush, so he decided to bag that idea.

The rented house was on fire. Fortunately, Ray had packed a duffel bag and stowed it in the shed. He grabbed the bag and checked his surroundings in case the fourth man had come back. No one was lurking outside, so he ran to the thicket where he'd hidden his motorcycle. He pulled it out. Then he took out his phone and called the number on the card Karen Wyatt had given him.

"Four men just tried to kill me," he said. "Where can I meet you?"

As soon as Karen told him the address, Ray headed there. He'd seen the fourth assassin disappear into the woods, so he didn't think he was being followed. That is why he didn't check to see if someone was tailing him. Zegda had posted Gabby Wright near Ray's house so he could report on the success of the hit team. Gabby told Walt about the shots and the explosion. Then he told him that Ray was alive and he was following him toward town.

CHAPTER THIRTY-FIVE

Walter Zegda had brought up a hit team of Disciples affiliates from the Bay Area. Derek Baines, the only survivor of the failed raid, limped through the woods as fast as his wounds let him. Every few steps, he looked over his shoulder to make sure that Castor wasn't tracking him. He didn't breathe easily until he was on the road with no Harley in sight. When he thought he was safe, he pulled into a side road and examined his wounds. A piece of wood had lacerated his leg and another had cut a groove through his cheek, but the wounds were superficial. There was a first aid kit in the car, and he dressed the wounds. Then he made the call he was dreading.

"It was a clusterfuck. Castor ambushed us. I'm the only one who made it out alive, and I got hit too."

"I can't believe you screwed this up," said Zegda. "There were four of you."

"Now there's only me, Walt. We lost some good men."

"Yeah, I'm sorry about that."

"I'm headed home, but I wanted to let you know what happened."

"I appreciate that, but I have one more job for you."

"No, I'm out of here."

"I'll pay triple what I paid for Castor."

There was dead air for a minute. "What's the job?"

"It's an attorney, and I need her dead before Castor can get to her. If you bag Castor too, I'll pay triple for both."

Karen called Morris Johnson as soon as Castor ended his call. Fifteen minutes later, he joined her in the lobby of the condo building.

"We need to get Castor someplace safe," Karen said. "I have a private jet waiting, and our security people are sending over a team to protect him."

"Good move. It would be too risky for Castor to fly commercial."

"What about Nikki Randolph?" Karen asked.

"Let's wait to see what Castor wants to do."

Fifteen minutes later, Karen and Morris saw Ray's Harley stop at the curb. They opened the door to the building and walked outside. Ray dismounted and walked toward them just as a car drove by at a slow speed.

"Gun!" Morris shouted as he pulled out his weapon.

Ray turned toward the street, and Derek Baines shot him. He fell on the sidewalk as Baines shifted his aim toward Karen. Morris opened fire, and Baines jerked his hand. The shot tore through the flesh in Karen's arm. Morris knocked her to the ground and sprayed Baines's car with bullets. As Baines sped away, Johnson memorized the number on his license plate.

"Are you hurt?" Morris asked.

"Don't worry about me. Check Castor. Get the name."

Morris ran to Ray. His breathing was ragged, and his eyes were closing. Karen saw Morris put his ear next to Castor's mouth as he said something. Then Morris sat back, and Ray stopped moving. Karen pressed a hand over her arm. Blood seeped through the rip in her jacket where the bullet had torn it. She ignored the pain and walked to her investigator.

"Did you get the name?" Karen asked.

Morris shook his head.

"He said something," Karen insisted. "What did he say?"

Morris turned toward her. His adrenaline had worn off, and he looked exhausted.

"I asked him for the name of the DA and he said, 'Starlight.'"

"Starlight? That's not a name."

"That's what he said."

"Do you think Nikki Randolph would know what he meant?"

"I can ask her."

Karen was lost in thought for a moment.

"Randolph is going to be very upset when she finds out that Castor is dead. There's a good chance that she'll blame me. We should give her an incentive to talk to you."

Muriel Lujack had lost a four-day trial. The judge had ordered a dinner break, and the jury didn't render its verdict until a little after eight. By the time she dragged herself into her bedroom, it was almost eleven. She was exhausted, but she couldn't sleep, because she kept replaying the trial in her head, searching for the moment it had gone wrong. By the time her brain finally ran out of gas, it was a new day.

Muriel overslept and didn't get up until eight. She showered before consuming a breakfast of toast and coffee while she read the news on her phone. She froze when she saw the headline. Then she scrolled down to the story about the shoot-out at Karen Wyatt's condo.

When she'd turned on her phone, she'd noticed that she had a voicemail. It was from Wyatt. She called immediately.

"Are you okay?" Muriel asked as soon as Karen answered. "The news feed said you were wounded."

"A bullet grazed my arm. It hurts, but there's no real damage."

"Why did you call me? I'd have thought there were a lot of other things you'd be doing."

"There are a million things. I'm on my way to police headquarters to give a statement. But something happened that you might be able to help me with."

"Shoot."

"That's a poor choice of words, given what happened."

"Sorry. So, how can I help?"

"You know Raymond Castor was killed at my condo?"

"Yes."

"He was going to tell me the name of the DA in your office who is working with the Disciples. When he was shot, Morris Johnson, my investigator, asked him for the name. He died before he could tell it, but he did say something, and we can't figure out what it means. I was hoping you might be able to solve the mystery."

"What did he say?"

"Starlight."

"What?"

"Starlight."

"I have no idea what that means."

"There's no DA with that name?"

"Not even close."

"Okay. Thanks. Think about it, and call me if you come up with something."

Muriel ended the call. Starlight. She rolled the word over in her head as she finished her breakfast, but she still had no idea what it meant when she left for work.

CHAPTER THIRTY-SIX

Audrey Packer and Chad Remington had been assigned to the Raymond Castor case as soon as the connection to the Lucifer's Disciples was made. When they arrived at Castor's house, they found firefighters dealing with the blaze, two dead men in the front yard, and the charred remains of a third man in the ruins of Castor's kitchen.

After leaving Castor's house, the detectives drove to Karen Wyatt's condo to talk to her and Morris Johnson. When they saw how exhausted they were and the wound in Wyatt's arm, the detectives agreed to put off taking their statements.

An APB had gone out with a description of the shooter's car and the license plate. On the way back to the station, the detectives learned that Derek Baines had been arrested and was being held for them in an interrogation room. They were at the head of the corridor that led to the room when they saw district attorneys Ellen Kaufman and Oscar Vanderlasky walking toward them.

"Hi, Ellen," Audrey said. "What are you doing here?"

"Oscar and I just finished talking to Derek Baines, the Disciple who shot Raymond Castor and Karen Wyatt."

"We got lucky," Vanderlasky said. "Baines was nabbed a few blocks from one of the garages the Disciples use as a chop shop. Baines and his car would have disappeared if he'd made it to the garage."

"Did you get anything out of him?" Chad asked.

"He says he doesn't know what we were talking about," Ellen said.

"We'll take a shot," Chad said. "We can compare notes."

"Sounds good," Ellen said.

"What the fuck!" Audrey fumed as soon as the DAs were out of hearing range. "They had no business talking to Baines before we did."

"What's done is done," Chad said, but it was clear that he was just as upset as his partner. "Let's see if we have better luck."

Before they started questioning Baines, the detectives watched him on the camera feed that let them see inside the interview room. The prisoner looked exhausted. His head drooped, and his eyes closed from time to time. When Packer and Remington walked in, Baines looked up.

"Which one of you is the good cop and which one is the bad cop?" he asked.

Chad smiled. "You watch too many police shows, Derek. We left our rubber hoses in our office, and we're both very nice cops." Chad handed Baines the cup of coffee he was holding. "See?"

Baines smiled. He was tired, but he wasn't nervous. It was obvious that he was no neophyte to police interrogation.

"Thanks for the coffee," Baines said.

"Are you hungry? I imagine shooting Raymond Castor and Karen Wyatt must have built up an appetite."

"Who?"

"Come on, Derek. You were ID'd by the guy who memorized your license plate."

Baines shrugged. "He must have made a mistake with some of the letters or numbers, because I don't know what you're talking about. I could go for a sandwich or a pizza."

"Which I would gladly trade you for the name of the person who paid for the hit on Mr. Castor. We've also run the prints of the dead Disciples at his house, and we know the four of you came up from Oakland. We're also pretty certain who asked you to kill Castor. But it would help us, and benefit you, if you helped us prove we have the right guy."

"I'd help if I could, but I really don't know what you're talking about."

"I guess you got your injuries by humping an oak tree," Audrey said. "The splinters the EMTs found in your wounds match the tree that was blasted to shit in Castor's side yard."

"Was it a rare tree? Because Oregon is famous for its varied foliage."

"A person who uses words like *varied* and *foliage* is no dummy. That's why we're going to get you some food and let you think about your situation while we talk to the DA about a deal that might keep you off death row."

CHAPTER THIRTY-SEVEN

Walter Zegda was usually calm and in control, so Wolf was surprised to see his friend pacing back and forth when he joined him on the deck of Zegda's house.

"What's wrong?"

"My DA called. They arrested Baines. He's at the police station."

"He won't talk."

"Don't be so sure, Wolf. The word I got was that he's playing dumb now, but he shot Wyatt. Like you said, she's not a nobody like Castor. She's an attorney. She made headlines when she was sprung from prison. Everyone knows who she is, which means that the cops will have to make her case a priority so they don't look like they're fucking her over again. We're talking aggravated murder and attempted aggravated murder with death row in Baines's future."

Wolf shrugged. "Let's assume that Baines names you. Where's the corroboration? Everyone else who hit Castor is dead. Our lawyers will argue he said what he said to avoid a murder charge."

"There were calls."

"On burner phones. Be cool and this will go away."

"What if Castor gave up the DA's name before he died?"

Wolf looked concerned. "That would be a problem."

Wolf shifted so he was between the rail and Zegda, who was about to reply when Larson's head exploded and showered him with brains, blood, and skull fragments.

Zegda had the reflexes of an exceptional athlete. He dropped to the ground just as another shot passed through the space where his head had been.

Packer and Remington were exhausted and ready to head home when they were told to drive to Walter Zegda's house. They parked in Zegda's driveway and walked onto his deck. The sun was rising behind Mount Hood, painting the sky scarlet red and bright orange. Audrey ignored the gore for a moment and took in the spectacular view.

"We're in the wrong business, Chad. We should have been drug dealers."

"It's not too late to change careers."

Audrey looked at the body sprawled on the deck surrounded by blood and skull fragments.

"There is a downside," she said.

"I don't think we have to ask the medical examiner if she has an opinion about the cause of death."

"I don't have a medical degree, but I think we can make a

good guess. And I'll bet the killer was in the woods below the house."

Remington and Packer could see officers searching the forest.

"We're not going to lack for suspects," Audrey said.

"Larson was killed by someone who is very good with a rifle."

"That narrows it down, but not by much. There are one or more ex-military in every rival gang, and every other person in Oregon hunts."

"I bet the Disciples affiliate in Oakland has someone who fits the profile, and they might be a little pissed about losing three men and having a fourth in custody, who is facing enough serious charges that he may be tempted to unburden himself."

"Don't forget the people who were laundering money through Zegda's businesses."

"You're talking about Cogen?"

"And the person who killed him."

"One thing, though. The person who killed Larson and tried to shoot Zegda must know Zegda very well," Chad said.

"Why do you say that?" Audrey asked.

"We've had people inside the Disciples, and they've all said that Zegda was really paranoid about surveillance. He never talked business in any tavern where the Disciples congregated, he picked different coffee shops for important meetings, he never discussed business in the Disciples' clubhouse, and he had his house swept for bugs every day. I'm betting Larson and Zegda were discussing the hit on Castor. The person who shot at them knew Zegda wouldn't talk about it inside his house. He was counting on Zegda talking to Larson on his deck. Which means that he had to know a lot about Zegda's habits."

"Good point," Audrey agreed. "You know, if they were talking about Baines, someone had to have tipped off Zegda that we had him."

"He has cops on his payroll," Chad said.

"There's a rumor that he still has a DA on it too."

They both remembered that Oscar Vanderlasky and Ellen Kaufman had talked to Baines earlier in the evening, but both detectives kept their suspicions to themselves.

"Let's talk to Mr. Zegda," Chad said.

The detectives found the leader of the Lucifer's Disciples sitting on a chair in a corner of the living room. He had wiped the gore off his face, but he was still dressed in the blood-spattered clothes he was wearing when someone tried to kill him.

Zegda's eyes were closed, and his head was resting against the top of the chair.

"Mr. Zegda," Chad said.

Zegda opened his eyes and stared at the detectives.

"I'm Chad Remington, and this is Audrey Packer. We're with Portland Homicide, and we'd like to talk to you about what happened tonight."

"Take a seat and ask away," Zegda said. He sounded exhausted.

"I understand that Mr. Larson was a good friend," Chad said.

"He was."

"I'm sorry for your loss."

"Not as sorry as the person who killed him will be," Zegda said.

"I understand your anger, but taking the law into your own hands will get you in a lot of trouble. You should let us handle this."

"Oh, you thought . . . No, no. I would never seek revenge for Wolf's death. That's a job for the authorities."

"That's good," Chad said, but he didn't believe a word of what Walter Zegda had just said.

"Do you have any idea of who the person is who shot Mr. Larson?" Audrey asked.

"We were talking on the deck. Then Wolf's head exploded. I dropped to the floor and crawled inside. So, I didn't see a thing."

"What about enemies?" Chad asked.

Zegda smiled. "Let's not play games. You know who I am and what I do. If I started telling you the names of people who would like to see me dead, we'd be here all week. And the list would include many of your acquaintances."

"I wouldn't be on that list," Chad said. "I will be honest. I'd love to see you behind bars, but I assure you that I am going to try my hardest to find the person who tried to kill you."

"I appreciate that. I know your and Detective Packer's reputations, so I know you're being honest."

"Will you tell us if you get a lead on the person who shot at you?"

Zegda flashed a humorless smile. "I'm very tired, and it's way past my bedtime. I gave a statement to the first responder, and I'd like to go to sleep now, if you're through asking questions."

"Of course. If we have any more questions, we'll get in touch."

Chad and Audrey gave Zegda their cards and walked outside. The sun was up, and the mountains rose behind Portland, their beauty a stark contrast to the carnage on the deck.

"I pity the person who killed Zegda's friend, if he gets his hands on him before we do," Audrey said.

"Amen," Chad answered.

CHAPTER THIRTY-EIGHT

Morris Johnson went to the office where Nikki Randolph worked and learned that she'd called in sick.

He had to ring Randolph's bell several times and knock twice before she opened the door.

"What do you want?" Randolph asked. Her speech was slurred, her breath reeked of cheap whiskey, and her eyes were bloodshot from crying.

"I'm really sorry about Ray-Ray," Morris said. "He died in my arms."

"He died because you and that bitch Wyatt killed him."

"We think Walter Zegda hired the man who shot Ray-Ray."

"And why did Walt send someone after Ray?" Randolph asked defiantly. "It's because he found out that you motherfuckers bailed him out."

"Nikki, we were going to fly him out of Portland with you on a private plane. We were going to save both of you when he was shot. Karen was shot too, and she still wants to help you."

"She can help me by killing herself," Randolph said as she started to shut the door.

"Karen wants to pay you. She knows it won't bring Ray-Ray back, but it might keep you safe."

"I don't want your blood money. Now get off my property."

"Nikki, Ray said something before he died. He said your name," Morris lied. "He wanted me to tell you that he loved you."

Tears welled up in Randolph's eyes, and her knees buckled. She grabbed the wall to keep from falling. Morris opened the door and helped Randolph to her couch. She dropped onto it, her eyes tightly shut, wailing.

"It's okay," Morris said. "He loved you, Nikki. You'll always have that."

Morris stopped talking and waited for Randolph to calm down. Eventually, she stopped crying. Her breathing slowed. Morris took an envelope out of his pocket. It was stuffed with hundred-dollar bills.

"This is for you."

Randolph didn't take the envelope, so Morris put it next to her on the couch. Randolph focused on the investigator. Her features morphed from sorrow to suspicion.

"What's the catch? What do I have to do for the money?"

"There is no catch. Miss Wyatt feels awful, because she feels responsible for what happened to Ray."

"There's always a catch. What does she want from me?"

"Nothing. Like I said, this is a gift. But I did have a question. You know that Zegda sent a hit squad to kill Ray?"

"I saw what happened at his house on TV."

"When he escaped, he called Miss Wyatt. We told him we were going to fly the two of you somewhere safe. When he was dying, he tried to tell me the name of the DA Zegda has on his payroll, but he was hurting too much. But he did say something that is puzzling me. After he said he loved you, he said 'Starlight,' and I have no idea what it means. Do you?"

Randolph flashed a bitter smile. "I knew there was a catch. The money is for the name."

"Absolutely not."

Randolph grabbed the envelope with the money and threw it at Morris. He let it bounce off him and drop to the floor. Randolph stood up.

"Get out."

"Nikki . . ."

"Get the fuck out of my house, or I'll call the cops. And about 'Starlight.' I have no fucking idea what that means, but if I figure it out, you can tell your boss I will never tell her."

CHAPTER THIRTY-NINE

The events of the past week had moved at warp speed. Billy Kramer had been murdered. There had been the shoot-out at Raymond Castor's house, his murder on the steps of Karen Wyatt's building, and the assassination of Wolf Larson. Then everything slowed down to a snail's pace. The police had no leads in the murder of Wolf Larson. Everyone thought that Zegda had murdered Kramer, but there was no way to prove it, so no one was spending any time on the case. Derek Baines had lawyered up and wasn't talking, and Karen still had no clue what "Starlight" meant.

The only positive entry on the plus side of Karen's ledger had been a visit from the doctor Karen had been seeing. Barry Clay had called to see if she was all right when he heard about the shooting. Then he had offered to cook her dinner at her place. When he showed up, he brought flowers, a Caesar salad, and the ingredients for spaghetti carbonara, which had been delicious.

By the end of the week, Karen was back in her office working on her other cases, but she felt like she was spinning her wheels. Jack Blackburn's trial was set to go in two weeks, but most of her prep for the case had been completed. None of her other cases were scheduled for trial soon, and many of them were in suspended animation while she waited for responses from opposing counsel. So, she was delighted when Morris Johnson walked into her office with a smile on his face and told her that he had some good news.

"I don't want you to get too excited, but I might have figured out a way to weaken Vanderlasky's case against Jack Blackburn."

"Tell me."

"I went to the tavern where Jack met Billy Kramer, and I showed the bartender who served everyone a photograph of the beer glass that was found at Cogen's place. He said it matched the glasses they use. He showed me a glass, and it was identical, but he said that a lot of bars use identical glasses. Then I crossed my fingers and I asked him my next question."

Morris told her what he'd discovered.

"That's fantastic!" Karen exclaimed.

Morris smiled. "That's why you pay me the big bucks."

Karen frowned. "We'll have to give Vanderlasky discovery."

Morris grinned. "I haven't written a report, so all we have to give him is our witness list with the witness's name and contact info. If Vanderlasky interviews her, he'll know what we know, but only if he asks the right questions."

CHAPTER FORTY

Chad Remington and Audrey Packer agreed that they should not accompany the Horans to Valerie Girard's office, so it was Francine who introduced her husband to the psychiatrist.

"Why don't you two take a seat on my sofa," Valerie said.

Horan sat down next to Francine. He looked very tense.

"What's going to happen, Dr. Girard?" the congressman asked.

"Since we're going to be working together, why don't you call me Valerie."

"Okay."

"Can I call you Tom?"

"Yes."

"Are you nervous about being hypnotized?" Valerie asked.

"A little."

"Everyone who is hypnotized for the first time is nervous,

so that shows that you're normal. And I'm glad you're open and honest with me. I promise to be open and honest with you. Anytime you're concerned about something or have a question, let me know. I want you to know everything that's going on. Now, tell me, have you ever seen someone being hypnotized?"

"On TV."

"The stuff you see on TV can be misleading. In the movies and television, the bad guys hypnotize a person and make them commit crimes, but you can't make a hypnotized person do something that they don't want to do. I'm going to use hypnosis to help you, not hurt you. I know you've gone through a terrifying experience. Francine tells me that you have nightmares. So, we're going to work together to get to the bottom of what's troubling you. Are you up for that?"

"Yes. I want to understand what happened to me."

"Good. Then let's get started. Francine, do you mind waiting outside? Tom needs to be free of distractions."

Francine put a reassuring hand on her husband's shoulder and went into the waiting room. As soon as the door closed behind her, Valerie told Horan to sit in an easy chair that was next to the sofa. When he was seated, she put a pillow behind his head and took a seat opposite him.

"Are you comfortable?"

"Yes."

"Good. Now I want you to try to relax while I tell you what's going to happen. There won't be any surprises." Valerie's tone was soothing and steady. "You'll notice that you may get a little drowsy as we proceed. This is normal. Each night when you go to sleep, you go through an experience that is like hypnosis. I want this to be a relaxing and pleasant experience. I'm not going to ask you any questions that will embarrass you, so make your mind passive and don't analyze your thoughts or experiences. Do you understand?"

"Yes."

"Good. Now why don't you put your hands palm down on your thighs. No, don't close your eyes. Keep watching your hands. If you concentrate on your hands, you will notice that you can observe them very closely.

"When you sit and relax, you begin to notice things that you've never noticed before. They have always happened when you relax, but you have never been aware of them. I am going to point them out to you.

"Tom, I want you to concentrate on all the feelings and sensations in your hands, no matter what they may be. Perhaps you may feel the heaviness in your hand as it rests on your thigh, or you may feel the pressure. Perhaps you may feel the texture of your pants as it presses against your palm or the warmth of your hand on your thigh. Maybe you will feel a tingling. No matter what the sensations are, I want you to observe them.

"Good, Tom," Valerie said after a few moments. "Keep watching your hand. See how quiet it is. How it remains in one position. There is motion there, but it is not noticeable yet. I want you to keep watching your hand. Your attention may wander from the hand, but it will always return to the hand, and you will keep wondering when the motion that is there will show itself.

"It will be interesting to see which of your fingers will move first. It may be the ring finger or the thumb. One of the fingers is going to jerk or move. You don't know which, so keep watching and you will notice a slight movement, possibly on the right hand. Then the thumb is jerking, just like that.

"As the movement begins, you will notice an interesting thing. Very slowly, the spaces between your fingers will widen. The fingers will move apart, and you will notice that the spaces between the fingers will grow wider and wider. They will move slowly apart. See how they spread. Slowly moving wider and wider.

"Good, Tom. You are doing fine. The fingers are so wide apart. And soon you will notice that the fingers want to arch up from the thigh. Notice how the index finger is lifting. As it does, the other fingers will want to follow upward, slowly rising, up, up.

"See how the fingers are rising now. As they lift, you will become aware of a feeling of lightness, so much so that the fingers will arch up and the whole hand will rise as if it feels like a feather, as if a balloon is rising up in the air, lifting, lifting up, up, pulling it higher and higher. The hand is so light. And as you watch, you will notice that your arm comes up, higher and higher.

"Keep watching the hand and arm rise, and you will soon become aware of how tired and drowsy your eyes become. And as your arm continues to rise, you will get tired and relaxed and sleepy, very sleepy. Your eyes will get heavy and your lids will want to close. And as your arm rises, you will feel more relaxed and sleepier and you will want to enjoy the peaceful, relaxed feeling of letting your eyes close and being asleep.

"Good, Tom. Go to sleep, just sleep. And as you sleep, you will feel tired and relaxed. I want you to concentrate on relaxation, a tensionless relaxation. Think of nothing else but sleep, deep sleep."

Valerie paused while Horan fell into a somnambulistic state.

"Now, Tom," she said after a while, "I want you to recall a very happy, satisfying experience. A very pleasant experience where you felt strong and good and when those who knew you would have been proud and pleased. Can you remember an experience like that?"

"Yes," Tom said.

"Tell me about it."

"When I won my election in college. And Millie was so proud of me, and Terrance was so excited."

"Tell me more about that day."

"I worked so hard, and I was so nervous when they started tallying the votes. Then they said I won."

"How did you feel at the precise moment you knew you'd won?"

"Like . . . Like I could float up to the ceiling, and Millie kissed me and Terrance clapped me on the back and we grabbed one another and danced in a circle."

"You are doing great, Tom. And there are many wonderful experiences in life. Can you remember a present you received that made you very happy? Something that happened in the recent past?"

"Francine."

"What about Francine?"

"She surprised me. She took me to a resort."

"Why was this special?"

"It was paradise. It was warm. We lounged on the beach and watched the waves and drank piña coladas."

"That sounds wonderful. Was it as wonderful as the way you shined at the UFO hearing?"

Horan tensed.

"Relax, Tom. Feel how peaceful and calm you are in your deep, restful sleep. Can you feel how safe and secure you are? How in control?"

"I . . ."

"Look at your hand and feel it drift up like a feather. Feel how light it is. Can you feel it floating?"

"Yes."

"Good. Now I want you to remember how good it felt to come back home as a hero, after the hearing. How did you feel?"

"It was good."

"What did Francine say when you came home?"

"She said I knocked the ball out of the park."

"When did she say that?"

"When she picked me up at the airport."

"Remember how good it felt to be praised by your wife."

Horan smiled.

"Were you still feeling good when you received a phone call later that day?"

"Yes."

"Who called?"

Horan stopped smiling. His shoulders tensed.

"Relax, Tom. You're in a safe place. Nothing can hurt you here while you are relaxed and sleeping deeply. Tell me who is calling."

"Terrance."

"See? Nothing hurt you, because you are safe and protected here. Watch your hand floating in air. Feel how comfortable and sleepy you are."

Horan's shoulders loosened, and his head sank into the pillow.

"We are going to take a trip. You will be safe and happy while we travel. We're driving to see your friend Terrance. Can you see the road?"

"Yes."

"You're such a good driver. So relaxed, in command. Is it easy to drive?"

"Yes."

"See how smooth and easy the ride is to Terrance's house. Can you see the house?"

"It's dark."

"Are you driving at night?"

"Yes."

"That's not hard for an expert driver. Can you stop the car?"

"Yes."

"Good. You're doing so well. Now that you are at your friend's house, what do you see?"

"It's dark, and . . . I'm nervous."

"Put away your anxiety. You are protected. You are in a safe place where no harm can come to you. See how your hand floats, light as a feather. Do you feel how calm the night air is, how peaceful?"

"Yes."

"Good, Tom. Now tell me, do you see anything outside the house?"

"I . . . There is something in the shadows as I drive to the house."

"What do you see?"

"It might be a car, but it is in the shadows, and I only see it out of the corner of my eye."

"Okay. Let's go inside. We can do that because we are just dreaming and we are asleep in a safe, relaxed place where you are in control, where nothing can hurt you. Do you feel how peaceful it is to be in a deep, relaxed sleep?"

"Yes."

"Good. This is just a dream. Let's go into the house in your dream. What do you see?"

"It's all dark, except for a light."

"Where is the light?"

"I think it's in the living room, but the light disappeared."

"How did that happen?"

"I . . . It just disappeared."

"Okay. Where are we going now?"

"Toward where the light was."

"You're doing great. You're in control of your dream. You are safe, and nothing can hurt you. When you reach where the light was, what do we do?"

"I turn it on and—" Horan stiffens.

"What do you see?"

"The thing. The monster. Then—" Horan curls up in his chair.

"It's okay. Concentrate on your hand. Let it rise. Breathe deeply. You are safe and secure. Nothing can hurt you."

Horan sank back into the armchair. His breathing slowed.

"We're almost there, Tom," Valerie said. "What do you see?"

"Someone is on the floor and . . . there's a mirror. Someone is behind me."

"Who is behind you?"

"Long, black hair."

"Is it a man or a woman?"

"I don't know."

"Try to see who is behind you."

"I . . . I can't." Horan shot up in the chair. He was breathing hard.

"It's okay. Relax. You're safe."

Horan was rigid and very agitated. Valerie decided that she would end the session.

"In a moment, I am going to ask you to wake up. When you do, you will feel happy and refreshed and free of fear."

Audrey Packer and Chad Remington met Valerie Girard in her office shortly after Congressman Horan and his wife left.

"What do you think happened to Horan on the night Cogen was murdered?" Audrey asked after Dr. Girard told them what Horan had said during their session.

"This is pure guesswork," Valerie answered.

"We understand."

"I think the house was dark, except for a light in the room where you found Terrance Cogen's body. I think the killer was in that room and turned off the light when Horan walked into the house. He probably called out for Cogen, alerting the killer.

"When Horan walked into the living room, the congressman turned on the light, saw Cogen's brutalized body, and was struck on the head by the killer."

"There's evidence to support that theory," Chad said. "The lab found blood from two different people on the statue the killer used to murder Cogen. Cogen's blood makes up the majority of the blood on the statue, but the lab identified Horan's blood too."

"So, how do you explain Horan's claim that he was abducted by aliens?" Audrey asked.

"It's possible that, in his subconscious, the light Horan saw when he flipped the switch in the living room for a second became the light that beamed him up to the ship."

"And the aliens?" Chad asked.

"The polar bear. He saw it for a fraction of a second, but filed it away in his subconscious as a huge, pale creature."

"And the killer?" Audrey asked.

"You told me that there was a mirror near the doorway of the living room?"

"Yes," Audrey answered.

"He may have gotten a glimpse of the person who hit him during the few seconds between turning on the light and being knocked unconscious. He saw long, black hair."

"A woman?"

"He couldn't tell me anything more."

"Thanks, Valerie," Chad said. "You've been an incredible help. Do you think you've helped Horan?"

"I gave him posthypnotic suggestions that may help him deal with his trauma."

"Are you convinced that he didn't kill Cogen?" Audrey asked.

"I don't think he did. I think the physical evidence suggests that someone hit him hard enough to cause his hallucinations."

"We can't thank you enough for your help," Chad said.

"I hope it does help catch the person who killed Terrance Cogen."

Neither detective said anything until they were outside. Then Audrey turned to Chad.

"Long, black hair suggests a woman."

Chad nodded. "What woman do we know who has long, black hair and would want to silence Terrance Cogen to keep him from telling the authorities the name of the person who really thought up the scams Cogen pulled?"

"A woman who could have met Walter Zegda in Mensa, a club in which they are both members," Audrey said.

"And who knows how to hunt."

CHAPTER FORTY-ONE

"We meet again," Rosemarie Cogen said when the door to the interrogation room opened and Audrey Packer and Chad Remington walked in. "Aaron, this is the charming couple who came to my penthouse with the sad news that Terrance had passed away."

"Hi, Aaron," Chad said to Aaron Jessup, the attorney Rosemarie had brought with her.

In legal circles, Jessup, a partner in one of Oregon's most prestigious firms, was considered to be the equivalent of a navy destroyer outfitted with nuclear warheads. Chad knew him when he was a US attorney who sent heads of drug cartels to federal prison.

"Afternoon, Chad, Audrey," Jessup said.

"I'm afraid we're going to convey more bad news during this visit," Chad said to Rosemarie.

Rosemarie smiled. "I'll have to make up my mind about that after you tell me why I'm here."

"Let's get the Miranda warnings out of the way," Chad said before going through them. "Do you understand your rights?"

"Yes, you did an excellent job explaining them."

"So, Chad, why is Mrs. Cogen here?" Jessup asked.

"We know she killed her husband," Audrey said.

"I didn't," Rosemarie answered.

"Do you have an alibi for the evening Mr. Cogen was killed?"

"Why, do you have a witness who can prove—I believe the legal requirement is 'beyond a reasonable doubt'—that I murdered Terrance?"

"Walter Zegda might be mad enough at you to testify."

"Who?" Rosemarie answered.

Chad took out a photograph of Walter Zegda and showed it to Rosemarie.

"Mr. Zegda is a fellow member of Mensa."

"Oh, Walt! I do know him, but not well. I'm sure we chatted a few times, but I don't remember any specific conversation. Why do you ask?"

"Walter Zegda is a notorious criminal and drug dealer who is the leader of a motorcycle gang called the Lucifer's Disciples. The same gang your dead husband was using to launder the profits from his scams."

"My goodness. I would never have guessed. Don't those people have tattoos and beards and dress in leather? Because Walt was always quite presentable when he attended our meetings."

"You can cut out the act, Rosemarie," Audrey said. "We know you and Zegda used your husband to steal millions. Then you killed him when an investigation started, because you knew he was weak and would implicate you as soon as he was arrested."

"I still haven't heard any evidence that links my client to her husband's murder," Jessup said. "Or to Walter Zegda, for that matter, other than their Mensa memberships."

Chad decided to bluff. "Thomas Horan was struck with the marble statue your client used to murder her husband. He's recovering his memory, and he saw your client in a mirror just before she struck him."

Jessup laughed. "Is this the same Thomas Horan who claims that he was abducted by aliens?"

Chad looked at Rosemarie. "You know, we will find the money and be able to link it to you."

"I don't see how you will be able to do that when I have no idea what happened to Terrance's ill-gotten gains. But waste the taxpayers' money if you must."

"I have a question for you," Audrey said. "Right now, we're executing a search warrant at your penthouse, your Dunthorpe estate, and the gun club where you practice. Do you think we'll find the rifle you used when you tried to murder Mr. Zegda and did kill Wolf Larson?"

"How sneaky. I could have saved you a lot of time. You won't find what you're looking for, because I never tried to shoot anyone. Why would I try to shoot Walt?"

"I think you knew we were closing in on him and were afraid he'd talk if he was arrested."

Jessup frowned. "I wouldn't have thought you two would pull a stunt like this. You could have asked Mrs. Cogen for permission to search, and she would have let you in without a warrant. She has nothing to hide."

Audrey looked at Rosemarie when she answered Jessup. "Then she won't have to worry about Mr. Zegda when he learns that you spent an hour talking to me at police headquarters."

CHAPTER FORTY-TWO

Rosemarie continued to maintain her innocence to her attorney while they walked to their cars, but her calm demeanor deserted her as soon as she was on her way to her apartment building. Walter was a dangerous psychotic who was prone to paranoia. She knew he admired her because she was one of the few people who was smarter than he was and just as ruthless, but she also knew that he could turn on her if he saw her as a threat.

By the time she parked in her reserved space, Rosemarie had decided to hire security guards. She was distracted by these thoughts and did not notice the van that was driving toward her until it was too late.

When Walter Zegda and Gabby Wright walked into the garage, the effects of the drug that had been injected when Rosemarie was kidnapped had worn off, and she was aware that she was tied to a chair that was resting on a large plastic sheet.

"Good afternoon, sunshine," Walter Zegda said.

"Untie me," Rosemarie demanded.

"Patience, Rosemarie. I'll loosen some of your bonds when we have our contest."

"What are you talking about?"

"I'll give you the details later. Right now, I'm more interested in finding out why you tried to shoot me."

"I didn't. What makes you think I'd do something like that?"

"Maybe because you wanted to make sure that I wouldn't tell the authorities that you offed Terrance to keep him from telling everyone where you're hiding the money he stole.

"And don't tell me you wouldn't be able to pick me off from the woods behind my house. The night we made love at your home in Dunthorpe, you showed me all the animals you'd bagged.

"I'm also interested in finding out what you told the police. Gabby followed you to police headquarters, so don't lie to me."

"Why would I tell them anything? They can't prove I've committed any crimes."

"That's what anyone who was about to be tortured would tell me."

"You're going to torture me?"

Zegda shrugged. "It's the only way I can be certain that you're telling me the truth. But first, we're going to have a contest that will decide whether you die quickly or slowly after I decide that I have all the information I need."

"Please, Walt, be reasonable. Why kill me? We make a great couple. Look at all the money we've made, and we're great in bed. Admit it. I'm the only woman you can see as an equal."

"Everything you say is true. I've never had better sex than I've had with you, and we've made a fortune together. But a relationship can't survive when one of the partners tries to kill the other one. I'm certain an advice columnist would agree with me. So, on to our contest. Gabby."

Gabby produced two Rubik's Cubes.

"I've been trying to break the world record for solving the cube for months. Sadly, I keep failing by fractions of seconds. Have you ever solved one of these babies?"

"Yes."

"Good. So, here's what we'll do. You get to pick the cube you want to work with, so you can be certain I'm not rigging the contest. Then Gabby will time us. Wolf used to work the clock, but you killed him, so Gabby is filling in. Wolf was my best friend, by the way. That gives me an added incentive to cause you a lot of pain. However, you will earn a quick death if you beat me. I looked up your IQ, and I know you scored ten points higher than I did, so you have an edge. But if you fail . . . I've been studying books on anatomy and torture, and I can promise you a very long and very unpleasant couple of months."

"Don't do this, Walt. I swear I never tried to kill you."

"If that's true, I will have made a terrible mistake. Now, let's get started. Pick your cube, Rosemarie."

"Gabby's right hand."

"Okay. Gabby, untie Rosemarie's hands and give her the cube."

Rosemarie shook out her hand to get the circulation back, Zegda flexed his fingers, and Gabby took out a stopwatch.

"Is everyone ready?" Gabby asked.

Rosemarie and Walt nodded.

"Ready, set, go!"

Rosemarie's and Zegda's fingers moved so quickly it was hard to see them. Then Rosemarie screamed, "Done!"

Zegda stopped and stared. He hadn't finished. "Gabby?" he asked.

"Three point one two."

"Son of a bitch," Zegda swore. "You did it. You broke the world's record. Congratulations. Sadly, no one will ever know. Gabby, take back the cube, and let's string our champion up to the rafters."

Gabby took two steps toward Rosemarie when the door to the garage crashed open and a team of police officers led by Audrey Packer and Chad Remington ran into the garage.

"How did you know I was here?" Rosemarie asked Audrey as she was being hustled out of the garage and into an ambulance to be checked by a paramedic.

"We thought that Zegda would come after you. So, you were followed as soon as you left police headquarters."

"Thank God! Zegda is insane. He was going to torture me, but he challenged me to a contest with a Rubik's Cube first. He said he would kill me quickly, after he tortured me, if I won."

"Did you?" Audrey asked. She was unsympathetic, and it showed in her tone of voice.

Rosemarie stared at her. "You can't still think I committed any crimes."

Audrey met Rosemarie's stare. "Now more than ever. Tell me, why do you think Zegda wanted to torture you if you had nothing to do with his criminal enterprises?"

"Maybe because he's stark staring mad."

"When we question Walter about his motivation for kidnapping you, we'll find out if he's crazy, if he's worried that you'll tell me about your involvement with your late husband's scams, or if he only knew you from brief chats at Mensa meetings."

"Audrey, I'm completely innocent. You have to believe me,"

Rosemarie said when they arrived at the ambulance and the EMTs took over.

The detective turned her back on Cogen and walked away.

"What do you think?" Chad asked his partner.

"She's dirty. I know it. She killed her husband, and she tried to kill Zegda so no one could tie her to Terrance's schemes."

"Assuming you're right, can we prove it?"

"I'm definitely going to try."

PART FIVE

THE STATE OF OREGON V. JACK BLACKBURN

CHAPTER FORTY-THREE

The night before she was going to give her opening statement in Jack Blackburn's case, Karen tossed and turned and woke up with a fuzzy head and no appetite. After using a cold shower to get her juices going, she scarfed down a bagel and a cup of strong black coffee. Then she headed for court.

Any case Karen tried generated a lot of press because of her celebrity status. Morris Johnson met her outside the courthouse and acted as a blocker as she plowed through the reporters, repeating, "No comment," as she went. When they made it through the gauntlet and entered the courtroom, Morris took a seat behind his boss so she could talk to him if she needed his help.

The stir in the courtroom alerted Oscar Vanderlasky to Karen's presence. Vanderlasky kept his eyes on his notes for his opening statement in the belief that ignoring opposing counsel psyched out his opponent and gave him a psychological edge. Karen thought the behavior was childish, and she stopped next to the prosecutor.

"Good morning, Oscar. Are you ready to rumble?"

Vanderlasky turned his head slowly and stared for a moment before answering, "I'm always ready. Especially when my case is bulletproof."

Karen smiled. "I guess we have different views of how this case will end."

The guards brought Jack to the defense table as soon as they saw Karen. She knew most of the jail personnel.

"Thanks, Charlie," she said to the guard as Jack took his seat next to Karen. Her client was still painfully thin, but he was wearing an expensive suit, shirt, and tie Karen had purchased for him, and he looked like an overworked junior associate instead of a jail inmate.

"How are you feeling?" Karen asked.

"Okay. I didn't get much sleep last night."

"That's normal. I didn't either. But I think you're going to feel much better pretty soon."

The bailiff rapped his gavel, and the Honorable Nathan Stark took his place on the dais and smiled at the jurors.

"Good morning. I hope you're rested and ready to hear the opening statements of counsel and the witnesses."

Then he shifted his eyes toward the prosecutor. "Are you ready to give your opening statement, Mr. Vanderlasky?"

"I am, Your Honor."

"Very well. You may proceed."

Vanderlasky stood slowly. Then he walked to the jury box with a confident stride and smiled at the jurors.

"Good morning, ladies and gentlemen, and thank you for taking time from your busy lives to serve on the jury in this very serious case. My name is Oscar Vanderlasky, and I am representing the people of Oregon in this very tragic trial.

"*State v. Jack Blackburn* is a murder case, and all murder cases involve a death, but the death in this case was unusually violent.

"You will hear that the victim, Terrance Cogen, was rendered unconscious by barbiturates that were in a milkshake he drank. Then, when he was completely defenseless, the defendant beat him to death with a heavy marble statue.

"When I was selecting you for this jury, I explained that some of the photographs you were going to see were very gruesome. I apologize in advance, but there is no way you will be able to understand how vicious and brutal this murder was unless you see the horrible way the defendant ended Mr. Cogen's life. And why was Mr. Cogen killed in such a horrible manner?"

Vanderlasky paused and shifted his gaze until he'd made eye contact with each juror.

"He was murdered for a car."

Vanderlasky paused again to emphasize the point.

"Terrance Cogen was wealthy, and he owned expensive automobiles. One of these cars was a 2019 Jaguar XJR575, which sells for roughly one hundred and twenty thousand dollars and is the type of car that is used to drive British royalty. Cynthia Woodruff was Terrance Cogen's housekeeper, and Billy Kramer was Mr. Cogen's chauffeur. Miss Woodruff will tell you that she and Mr. Kramer met the defendant for drinks at the Clinton Street Tavern. After a while, Miss Woodruff decided to go home. Mr. Kramer had driven the Jaguar to the tavern, but he told the defendant that he was too intoxicated to drive and asked the defendant to take Miss Woodruff home. The defendant agreed. And that's when the trouble started.

"Miss Woodruff will tell you that the defendant was stunned when he saw the car he was going to drive. During the drive to Miss Woodruff's apartment, he raved about the car and couldn't stop talking about it.

"The Jaguar was reported stolen. A few days after Mr. Cogen was beaten to death, the defendant was still driving the Jaguar when the police officers McDowell and Wheeler stopped him. When the officers asked him how the Jaguar came into his possession, he claimed that Billy Kramer lent him the car and he was trying to find Mr. Kramer to return it. The problem with this story is that the car's registration was in the glove compartment and it had Mr. Cogen's name and address on it. When the arresting officer pointed this out to the defendant, he made a lame excuse about not having thought to look at the registration to ascertain Mr. Cogen's address.

"Also in the glove compartment was Mr. Cogen's wallet. The crime lab examined bloodstains on the wallet, and a witness will tell you that the blood is Mr. Cogen's.

"Now, the defendant claims that he never went to Mr. Cogen's house, but we know that is a lie. How do we know? Mr. Cogen was beaten to death in his living room. The crime lab technicians found a beer glass on an end table in the living room near the victim. They discovered fingerprints on that glass. A witness will tell you that the prints belong to the defendant, who claims that he was never at Mr. Cogen's house. Unfortunately for him, the beer glass with his fingerprints on it place him, beyond a reasonable doubt, in the room where he callously beat a defenseless man to death. Thank you."

Vanderlasky turned his back to the jury so they couldn't see the self-satisfied smirk on his face, which he directed at Karen.

"Miss Wyatt," the judge said when Vanderlasky was seated.

Karen walked to the jury box. She shook her head and looked disappointed.

"Good morning. My name is Karen Wyatt, and I have the honor of representing Jack Blackburn, a man who is completely innocent of the charges that have been brought against him.

"When Mr. Vanderlasky told you what the evidence in this

case would show, I kept waiting for the rest of the story, but he must have lost his notes, because he left out so many important facts.

"The prosecutor didn't tell you why Billy Kramer asked Jack Blackburn to meet him and Miss Woodruff at the Clinton Street Tavern. He asked my client to meet him at the tavern so he could frame him for Terrance Cogen's murder. Miss Woodruff will tell you that Mr. Kramer told her that—"

Vanderlasky sprang to his feet. "Objection, Your Honor. May we have a sidebar?"

Judge Stark looked annoyed, but he nodded.

"Let's have the jurors step out so we can put this on the record," the judge said.

"What is your objection, Mr. Vanderlasky?" the judge asked as soon as the door to the jury room closed.

"Billy Kramer is dead, so he can't testify or be cross-examined. Anything Miss Woodruff testifies to that she claims Mr. Kramer told her that is introduced to prove the truth of the statement would be hearsay and inadmissible."

"Miss Wyatt?" the judge said.

In other trials with Vanderlasky, Karen had noticed that he did not have a comprehensive knowledge of the rules of evidence. She'd hoped that he would be too lazy to research some of the key legal issues in Jack's case, and he was proving that her confidence in his incompetence was well placed. She handed Vanderlasky and the bailiff a memorandum she had prepared.

"I guess Mr. Vanderlasky hasn't read the exceptions to the rule that excludes hearsay, which I detail in my memo," Karen said. "Statements against a person's interest are admissible. Miss Woodruff will testify that Mr. Kramer told her that he gave the car to my client to frame him for Mr. Cogen's murder. Giving the car to Mr. Blackburn under those circumstances is arguably theft, and framing him for a crime he didn't commit would, at least, be obstruction of justice. Those statements could subject Mr. Kramer to criminal liability, and Mr. Blackburn could sue him, which would open Mr. Kramer up to a suit for tort liability. So, the statements are against Mr. Kramer's interest."

Vanderlasky started to speak, but the judge cut him off and read the memo.

"Miss Wyatt is correct," the judge said when he finished reading. "If Miss Woodruff testifies about these statements, I will admit them over a hearsay objection. Let's bring the jury back."

Vanderlasky looked furious. Karen kept a smile off her face.

"As I was saying," Karen continued when the jurors were seated, "Mr. Kramer knew that Jack Blackburn loved cars, and he guessed that Mr. Blackburn would go nuts if he had a chance to drive the 2019 Jaguar XJR575, so he told Miss Woodruff to wait for an agreed-upon amount of time before saying that she wanted to go home. Mr. Kramer faked being intoxicated so he could have my client drive the Jag.

"When Miss Woodruff left with Mr. Blackburn, she told him to drive to what she told him was her apartment, but it was far away from where she lived. Sometime after Mr. Blackburn drove away, Mr. Kramer picked up Miss Woodruff in her car. Then he drove to Red Rim, Arizona, where he was hiding when the authorities arrested him.

"The first step in Mr. Kramer's plan to frame Mr. Blackburn for the murder of Terrance Cogen was getting him to drive the Jag, then disappearing from the bar so he couldn't give it back. But Mr. Kramer wasn't through with his plan to cause my client irreparable harm. He admitted to Miss Woodruff that he called the police in Portland pretending to be Terrance Cogen and reported that the Jaguar had been stolen.

"Now, the prosecutor did tell you that Mr. Cogen was rendered unconscious by barbiturates that were in a milkshake he drank. Mr. Cogen was a recovering alcoholic who drank milkshakes whenever he had the urge to drink alcohol. Mr. Kramer knew that because he used to be Mr. Cogen's houseman and made the milkshakes for him on occasion.

"Mr. Vanderlasky also neglected to tell you that Mr. Cogen was being investigated by state and federal authorities for conducting various fraudulent schemes in which he stole money from many people, costing some of them their life savings. These victims would have a motive for revenge.

"A 2019 Jaguar XJR575 is not a dull gray Toyota. It is a very unusual-looking car. The prosecutor would have you believe that Jack Blackburn murdered Terrance Cogen for a car he would never have been able to keep for very long. The absolute proof of that is the fact that Mr. Blackburn was arrested driving the car within days of Mr. Kramer reporting it stolen. You will have a massive reasonable doubt about whether Mr. Blackburn would murder someone for a car he would never possess for long.

"You will also wonder why Mr. Blackburn, who stayed in Portland, is a better suspect in Mr. Cogen's murder than Mr. Kramer, who ran away from Portland to Arizona on the day Mr. Cogen was murdered and hid from the police."

Karen paused and looked at each juror.

"I'm going to sit down now and let you hear the evidence. And I am confident that when you have heard all the evidence, you will have no doubts that my client is completely innocent and the victim of a vicious frame-up. Thank you."

CHAPTER FORTY-FOUR

Judge Stark ordered a brief recess after Karen and Vanderlasky finished giving their opening statements. When court reconvened, Vanderlasky called Dr. Sally Grace, the medical examiner who established that death occurred in the early evening, two days before the body was discovered.

"Was the defendant arrested two days after Mr. Cogen was murdered?"

"Yes."

"What caused Mr. Cogen's death?"

"Blunt force trauma to his head."

"Multiple blows with a heavy object?"

"Yes."

"I'm showing the witness a marble statue of the famous sculptor Rodin's *The Thinker* that was recovered near Mr. Cogen's body, and I'd like it marked as State's exhibit seven. Dr. Grace, are there bloodstains on this statue?"

"Yes. Several."

"Could this be the murder weapon?"

"I'm certain that it is."

"Was Mr. Cogen conscious or unconscious when he was beaten to death?"

"A toxicology screen of Mr. Cogen's stomach contents established that he had been rendered unconscious by barbiturates that had been administered in an ice cream milkshake."

"Did you learn that Mr. Cogen was a recovering alcoholic who regularly drank milkshakes so he wouldn't drink alcohol?"

"Yes."

"No further questions, Your Honor."

"Dr. Grace," Karen said, "you told the jurors that Mr. Cogen died from blunt force trauma caused by blows from a stone statue discovered at the murder scene and that there were several bloodstains on the statue."

"Yes."

"Was the blood from more than one person?"

"Yes."

"Was some of the blood from Mr. Cogen?"

"Yes."

"Was the other blood my client's?"

"No."

"Whose blood was it?"

"A man named Thomas Horan."

"Is Mr. Horan a United States congressman?"

"Yes."

"Thank you."

The prosecutor called Portland police officer Brady McDowell. Officer McDowell identified the car the defendant was driving from a photograph. Then he told the jury how enthusiastic the defendant was about the 2019 Jaguar XJR575. After that, he testified about what Jack Blackburn said about meeting Billy Kramer in the Clinton Street Tavern, driving Cynthia Woodruff home, and not finding Kramer when he tried to return the Jaguar. Officer McDowell recounted what Jack had said after being shown the registration with Cogen's name and address. Finally, he related what Blackburn said after being shown Cogen's bloodstained wallet. Then Vanderlasky had McDowell tell the jurors about the discovery of Terrance Cogen's body.

During a short cross-examination, Karen established that her client had been cooperative and seemed surprised when he was arrested.

"The State calls Inez Castro," Vanderlasky said when McDowell was excused.

A slim, middle-aged woman with curly black hair and blue eyes that were shielded by wire-rimmed glasses took the stand.

"Mrs. Castro, how are you employed?"

"I'm a forensic specialist at the Oregon State Crime Lab."

"Were you part of a group of forensic experts that worked the murder scene at Terrance Cogen's mansion?"

"I was."

"Did you examine a wallet that contained a credit card belonging to Terrance Cogen that was found in his 2019 XJR575 Jaguar?"

"Yes."

"Were there bloodstains on the wallet?"

"There were."

"Were you able to match the blood to a person?"

"Yes."

"Whose blood was it?"

"I matched it to the deceased, Terrance Cogen."

"Were there fingerprints on the wallet?"

"Yes."

"Were any of them the defendant's prints?"

"Yes."

"Mrs. Castro, did you take custody of a beer glass that was found near the deceased body?"

"I did."

Vanderlasky picked up an evidence bag containing the beer glass.

"I'd like this beer glass entered into evidence as State's exhibit five."

"No objection," Karen said.

"Is this the beer glass you found near Mr. Cogen's dead body?"

"Yes."

"Were you the expert who found latent fingerprints on the beer glass?"

"Yes."

"Is it a fact that no two people have the same fingerprints?"

"No one has ever found two people with identical prints."

"Were you able to match the fingerprints found on the beer glass to a person?"

"Yes."

"Who was that person?"

"Jack Blackburn."

"The defendant?"

"Yes."

"No further questions."

"Miss Wyatt?" Judge Stark said.

"Thank you, Your Honor. Mrs. Castro, isn't one of the guiding principles of crime scene investigation that a criminal will always leave some trace evidence that links him to a crime scene when he commits a crime?"

"Yes."

"Now, you found Mr. Blackburn's fingerprints on a beer glass at the scene?"

"Yes."

"If we don't count the prints found on the beer glass, please tell the jury how many of Mr. Blackburn's prints were found at the Cogen estate?"

"The only prints we found were on the glass."

"So, your answer is none."

"Yes."

"I assume you found traces of Mr. Blackburn's DNA all over the place."

"No. We didn't find any of his DNA at the estate."

"What about footprints, hair, and other trace evidence? Surely you found some of these things at the murder scene."

"We did not."

"Mrs. Castro, is it safe to say that there would be no evidence whatsoever connecting Jack Blackburn to the scene of Terrance Cogen's murder if the beer glass did not exist?"

"That is correct."

"No further questions, Your Honor."

"Any more witnesses, Mr. Vanderlasky?"

"The State calls Cynthia Woodruff."

Cynthia Woodruff looked like she would have preferred being anyplace other than the witness-box. Her voice shook when she took the oath, and she glanced at the jurors quickly, then looked away.

"Miss Woodruff," Vanderlasky asked, "did you know Terrance Cogen?"

"Yes. I worked in his house. I was his housekeeper."

"Did you know Billy Kramer?"

"Yeah. He was Mr. Cogen's chauffeur and houseman."

"Have you met the defendant, Jack Blackburn?"

"Just that one time."

"Was that at the Clinton Street Tavern?"

"Yes."

"Did the defendant drive you home from the tavern?"

"It wasn't to my home."

"But when you left, it was in a car driven by the defendant?"

"Yes."

"Was this a car that the murder victim, Terrance Cogen, owned?"

"Yes."

"I am showing you a picture of a Jaguar XJR575, which has been marked as State's exhibit fifteen. Is this the car you drove in with the defendant?"

"Yes."

"Where was the car parked?"

"It was in a parking garage a block or so from the tavern."

"How did the defendant react when he saw the car?"

"He . . . he got very excited."

"Did he talk about how fabulous the car was?"

"He wouldn't stop talking about it. He raved about the car all the time I was in it."

"Thank you, Miss Woodruff. I have no more questions."

"Any cross, Miss Wyatt?" Judge Stark asked.

"A little, Your Honor. Miss Woodruff, other than at the tavern and the ride from the tavern, had you ever met Jack Blackburn?"

"No."

"So, you never saw him at Mr. Cogen's estate?"

"No."

"Was the evening you met Mr. Blackburn the evening Mr. Cogen was murdered?"

"Yes."

"Please tell the jury why you met Mr. Blackburn."

Cynthia told the jurors that Billy Kramer had asked her to

drive her car to the Clinton Street Tavern, where they were going to meet Jack. Then she told the jurors that Kramer had instructed her to say that she wanted to go home when he gave her a cue. Karen had her tell the jurors that she gave Jack a false address as her apartment and how Kramer had picked her up and driven her to Red Rim, Arizona, where they had hidden in a motel until they were arrested.

"Miss Woodruff, how long would you estimate the time interval was between leaving the tavern with Mr. Blackburn and the time Mr. Kramer picked you up?"

"It must have been about an hour, because I was getting upset when Billy didn't come right away."

"Did you think he might have forgotten you?"

"It entered my mind."

"Let me ask you a question, and take your time before answering. Did Billy Kramer have enough time to drive from the tavern to Mr. Cogen's estate and then drive to the place you were waiting in the time it took you to drive to the place where Mr. Blackburn left you and the time Mr. Kramer picked you up?"

Cynthia's brow furrowed. After a few moments, she said, "He could have done it."

"At some point when you were with Mr. Kramer in Arizona, did he tell you why he wanted to give Mr. Blackburn the Jag?"

"Yes."

"What did he tell you?"

"He said that Mr. Cogen was dead, murdered."

"Did you know that before Mr. Kramer told you?"

"No! It scared the hell out of me."

"What did Mr. Cogen's murder have to do with letting Mr. Blackburn drive the 2019 Jaguar XJR575?"

"Billy said he wanted to frame Jack for the murder so no one would think he did it."

"What was his plan?"

"He knew Jack was crazy about cars and would be excited when he learned that he could drive the Jag."

"What was the rest of Mr. Kramer's plan?"

"It was awful. I told him so. He was going to disappear from the tavern so Jack wouldn't be able to return the car. He figured that Jack would want to keep driving it. Then—and here's the worst thing he did—he called the cops and pretended to be Mr. Cogen and reported the car stolen."

"Your Honor, I would like to play the 911 recording I have marked as Defense exhibit one for the jury."

"Mr. Vanderlasky?" the judge asked.

Vanderlasky looked uncomfortable, but he answered, "No objection."

"911, what is your emergency?" were the first words the jury heard when the recording played.

"This is Terrance Cogen. I own a 2019 Jaguar XJR575 car, license IRULE. It's been stolen."

Karen stopped the recording.

"Do you know what Terrance Cogen sounds like?"

"Of course. I spoke to him every day."

"Was that Terrance Cogen reporting the theft?"

"No, that was Billy Kramer."

"We've heard testimony that Mr. Cogen was a recovering alcoholic who drank milkshakes when he had an urge to drink alcohol. Did you know about this habit?"

"Yes."

"Did Mr. Kramer?"

"Yes."

"Did Mr. Kramer make milkshakes for Mr. Cogen?"

"Frequently."

"No further questions, Your Honor."

"Mr. Vanderlasky?"

"Thank you, Judge Stark. Miss Woodruff, isn't it true that you were very angry with Mr. Kramer?"

"Definitely."

"Were you and Mr. Kramer lovers?"

"Yeah."

"Were you staying in a low-rent motel when you were arrested?"

"Yes."

"Were you very angry that he made you hide out in a place like that for several days?"

"Yes."

"In fact, you were so angry at Mr. Kramer that you cut a deal with the police and my office, where you would get immunity from prosecution if you testified against Billy Kramer."

"Yes."

"Mr. Kramer is dead, isn't he?"

"Yes."

"So, you can make up any story you want to and he can't defend himself?"

"What I said is what happened."

"According to you, a woman who hated Mr. Kramer."

"I'm not lying."

"So you say. No further questions."

"No redirect," Karen said.

"Any more witnesses, Mr. Vanderlasky?"

"No, Your Honor. The State rests."

"I assume you have some motions, Miss Wyatt."

"I do."

"Let's take our lunch break and reconvene at one thirty, and I'll hear them then."

"How are we doing?" Jack Blackburn asked.

Karen could see that he was very nervous, so she put her hand on his shoulder and gave it a quick squeeze.

"I think we're going to blow the DA's case out of the water when we put on our case."

"Am I going to have to testify?"

"I haven't decided yet. Let's wait and see how the evidence shakes out."

CHAPTER FORTY-FIVE

When court reconvened, Karen made a motion for judgment of acquittal, which she knew she would lose. In order to win and have the judge throw out Vanderlasky's case, she had to convince Judge Stark that no jury would be able to convict Jack Blackburn if the evidence was viewed in the light most favorable to the State. Karen knew that the beer glass placed her client at the scene and possession of the Jag provided a motive for murder.

"Call your first witness, Miss Wyatt," the judge said after denying her motion and having the jury brought in.

Karen called the district attorney who was investigating Terrance Cogen's criminal activities and established that many of the investors in his scheme had lost money and that there had been death threats aimed at Cogen.

"Mr. Blackburn calls Morris Johnson," Karen said.

"Mr. Johnson," Karen asked after Johnson took the oath to tell the truth and was seated in the witness stand, "how are you employed?"

"I'm the investigator at your law firm."

"What did you do before I hired you?"

"I was a detective in the Portland Police Bureau."

"With regard to this case, did I ask you to drive your car to the Clinton Street Tavern?"

"Yes."

"Why did I do that?"

"You wanted me to see how long it would take to drive from the tavern to the estate of Mr. Terrance Cogen, and from the estate to the place where Billy Kramer met Cynthia Woodruff when he drove her to Arizona on the evening that Mr. Cogen was murdered."

"Please tell the jury how long it took to drive from the tavern to the Cogen estate and then to the point where Mr. Kramer rendezvoused with Miss Woodruff."

"I drove at the speed limit. The trip took roughly one hour."

"Thank you. No further questions."

"Mr. Vanderlasky?" the judge asked.

"I have no questions for this witness, Your Honor."

"Any more witnesses, Miss Wyatt?"

"Yes, Your Honor. Mr. Blackburn calls Lenore Watkins."

A heavyset woman in her early thirties entered the courtroom and walked to the witness-box where she took the oath. Oscar Vanderlasky looked down at his witness list and shuffled through his notes.

"Miss Watkins, how are you employed?" Karen asked.

"I'm a waitress at the Clinton Street Tavern."

Vanderlasky frowned. He remembered seeing the name, but he didn't see a report that outlined what the witness was going to say.

"Have I told you the date that a man named Terrance Cogen was murdered?"

"Yes."

"Were you working at the tavern that night?"

"I checked, and I was."

"Did you see a woman named Cynthia Woodruff just now when she left the courtroom?"

"Yes."

"Had you seen her before?"

"Yes, on the night that Mr. Cogen was murdered."

"Do you see anyone else in the courtroom who was at the tavern that night?"

The witness pointed at Jack Blackburn. "That man, Woodruff, and another man were at a table I served."

"May I approach the witness?" Karen asked the judge.

"You may."

"I'm showing Miss Watkins a photograph of Billy Kramer. Do you recognize him?"

"He was the third person at the table."

"Do you remember the order in which the three people left the tavern?"

"I do."

"How did they leave?"

"Mr. Blackburn and Miss Woodruff left together. Shortly after they left, Mr. Kramer paid the tab. Then he left."

"Why are you able to remember the order?"

"Because of what happened after Mr. Kramer left."

"Tell the jurors what happened."

"I was busy with another customer when Mr. Kramer left. I went to the table to clear it. Mr. Kramer didn't leave a tip, which upset me. Then I noticed that a beer glass was missing."

"How do you know it was missing?"

"Miss Woodruff only had a glass of wine. Mr. Kramer

had ordered a pitcher of beer. Mr. Blackburn and Mr. Kramer each had a beer glass, and they were refilling their glasses from the pitcher. When it was empty, Mr. Kramer ordered a second pitcher. When I brought the bill, there was a beer glass where Mr. Kramer was sitting and another glass where Mr. Blackburn had sat. When I came back to the table to clear it, the beer glass in front of Mr. Blackburn's seat was gone."

"Why do you remember this?"

"I told my boss that I thought Kramer took a glass. I didn't want to get charged for it."

Karen gave the witness State's exhibit five. "Does this look familiar?"

"It looks like the beer glasses we use at the tavern."

"Does it look like the beer glass Mr. Blackburn drank from, the one that disappeared?"

"Yes."

"Your witness, Mr. Vanderlasky," Karen said, her tone neutral and no trace of a smile on her face.

Vanderlasky looked flustered. He took some time pretending to look at his notes while he struggled to think up questions for the witness who had crippled his case.

"Miss Watkins, you said that State's exhibit five resembles the glass you use in the tavern."

"Yes."

"Isn't it true that many bars and taverns in Portland use this type of glass?"

"Yes."

"And they're sold in stores around the city?"

"I've seen them in some stores."

"You can't swear that this glass is the glass Mr. Blackburn drank from at the Clinton Street Tavern, can you?"

"No, it just looks like it."

"No further questions."

"Miss Wyatt?" the judge asked.

"Can we take a brief recess?"

"Will fifteen minutes do?"

"It should."

Karen walked to a corner of the courtroom where she and Morris Johnson would not be overheard.

"Should I call Jack?" she asked.

"No. All he can do is say he didn't kill Cogen. Vanderlasky can use his prior statements to rattle him. He'd look bad."

"That's what I think."

"And I think you poked a lot of holes in Vanderlasky's case," Johnson said.

"Enough to raise a reasonable doubt without putting Jack on the stand?" Karen asked.

"More than enough."

"Should we call Horan? He told the shrink that he saw a person with long, black hair in the mirror. Jack has blond hair, but Rosemarie Cogen is taller than Jack, has a motive for killing her husband, and has long, black hair."

Johnson shook his head. "Oscar would tear the congressman to shreds."

Karen sighed. "I agree."

"Any more witnesses?" Judge Stark asked when court reconvened.

"No, Your Honor. The defense rests."

"Then do you have any motions before I bring back the jury so they can hear closing arguments?"

"I do. Now that all the evidence is in, I want to renew my motion for a judgment of acquittal. It is our position that there is so much reasonable doubt about Jack Blackburn's guilt that no reasonable jury could find him guilty, even if you took the evidence in the light most favorable to the State.

"Let's look at the sequence of events on the evening Mr.

Cogen was killed. Miss Woodruff's evidence proves that Billy Kramer lured my client to the Clinton Street Tavern to frame him for the murder of Mr. Cogen. That means that Kramer knew Cogen was dead before he lured Jack Blackburn to the tavern and before Mr. Blackburn got possession of the Jaguar.

"Now, the only evidence placing Mr. Blackburn near Mr. Cogen's body is the beer glass. But Lenore Watkins's testimony provides overwhelming evidence that Mr. Kramer took the glass from the tavern as part of his plan to frame Mr. Blackburn, and Miss Woodruff told you that there was time for Mr. Kramer to leave the tavern with the glass, plant it near Mr. Cogen's body, and drive to the place where Kramer picked up Miss Woodruff so they could flee to Arizona.

"Then there are the barbiturates that were used to sedate Mr. Cogen. Mr. Kramer knew that Mr. Cogen habitually drank milkshakes. How did Mr. Blackburn know that? There is no evidence that he ran in Mr. Cogen's social circle, and there is no evidence, except for the beer glass, that he was ever at the estate.

"The person who is most likely to have killed Mr. Cogen is Billy Kramer, the person who admitted to framing my client and who went on the run."

Oscar Vanderlasky started to stand.

"Mr. Vanderlasky," Judge Stark said, "before you say anything, I have something to say to you. It is very difficult to win a motion for a judgment of acquittal, but I am going to have to think long and hard about what I am going to do in this case. I can tell you that if I were on this jury, I would definitely have a reasonable doubt about Mr. Blackburn's guilt on the murder charge.

"I am going to suggest that you talk to Miss Wyatt about a way to resolve this case before you answer her argument for this motion. So, I am going to recess court and clear the courtroom so you two can talk."

"What's happening?" Jack asked as the spectators left the courtroom.

Karen leaned over and spoke softly so no one could hear what she said. "The guards are going to take you upstairs while I talk to Mr. Vanderlasky and try to convince him to drop the murder charge."

"That would be great."

"Keep your fingers crossed."

Karen signaled the guards, and they escorted Jack out of the court and back to the courthouse jail.

Karen had been watching Vanderlasky, and she could tell that he was upset. She detested the prosecutor, and she would love to rub his nose in the fact that a competent prosecutor would have found out the truth about the beer glass before going to trial, just the way he would have figured out the importance of the lamp in Laurie Post's case. But Karen wasn't going to do that. No case she handled was ever her case. They were her clients' cases, and her job was to save her clients, not exact revenge. She opted for diplomacy. Karen pulled a chair next to the prosecutor's table. Vanderlasky turned toward her.

"You think you're so smart," he spat out.

"No, Oscar. Morris just kept digging, and we got lucky. If you take a minute to think about what just happened, you'll realize that you got lucky too. How would you feel if you convicted Jack, then you found out that he was innocent?"

Karen didn't think that Vanderlasky would spend a nanosecond regretting the conviction of an innocent person, but she pretended that she thought he would.

"I still think your guy killed Cogen, but I'll give Blackburn a break and let him plead to manslaughter."

"Didn't you listen to the judge? He's ready to dismiss all the charges. Your only chance of convicting Jack of murder was the beer glass, and that won't work anymore."

"What do you want, Wyatt?" Oscar asked.

"You're going to look good if you drop the charges in the interest of justice."

"You want this all to just go away?"

"Jack's gone through a lot."

"Jack is a thief. He would have kept that car forever if he hadn't been arrested."

"You're probably right, but life in prison is a pretty steep price to pay for boosting a car."

Karen let Vanderlasky think. She knew he'd heard the judge, and she gave him time to come around.

"I'll dismiss the murder charge. But Blackburn has to cop to the theft charge."

"That sounds fair. Do you want to do time served on the theft and probation? You'll sound great when I tell the reporters how you believed that this was the best way to serve justice."

Half an hour later, Karen and Vanderlasky told Judge Stark that they had arrived at a plea agreement that Mr. Blackburn had accepted.

"What have you two decided?" the judge asked when they were on the record.

Karen let Oscar Vanderlasky save face by presenting the plea agreement as something he had proposed.

"Your Honor, in the interests of justice, I have offered to dismiss the charge of murder in exchange for a plea of guilty to the count in the indictment that charges Mr. Blackburn with the theft of the Jaguar automobile. Additionally, we have agreed that the defendant should receive a sentence of five years on the theft charge, but you should place him on probation instead of having him imprisoned and give him credit for the time he has served in jail awaiting trial."

"Is your client willing to accept Mr. Vanderlasky's offer, Miss Wyatt?" the judge asked.

"Mr. Blackburn will accept Mr. Vanderlasky's offer, and I want to commend him for being open-minded and putting the interests of justice at the forefront in this prosecution."

"Very well. Mr. Blackburn, do you understand what has just happened?"

"Yes, sir. I'm not going to be charged with murder anymore, and I admit that I knew I didn't have any right to drive the Jaguar and should have brought it back to Mr. Cogen, who I knew owned it, because of the registration."

"I will accept your plea, Mr. Blackburn, and the sentencing recommendation. Mr. Blackburn, you are lucky to have the assistance of an excellent lawyer and a prosecutor who wanted to see justice served."

Vanderlasky left the courtroom. When the reporters stopped him, he put a spin on his decision to drop the murder charge that made him sound like Mother Teresa and Martin Luther King Jr. rolled into one.

When Karen spoke to the press, she heaped praise on her adversary, even though he had dug in his heels during their negotiations, only giving in when she reminded him that there was a good chance that Judge Stark would grant her motion and declare a mistrial on the auto theft case that would leave him with nothing.

"I'm glad that's over," Karen said as she and Morris Johnson headed back to the office.

"You did a great job."

"No, Morris. You won this case when you found Lenore Watkins. Her testimony destroyed Oscar's case."

"Why don't we agree that we're a pretty good team?"

Karen smiled. "It's a deal."

"So," Morris asked. "Who do you think killed Terrance Cogen?"

"I have no idea, and it's not my problem anymore."

"Aren't you curious? I lean toward Kramer. Though I can't figure why he'd do it."

"There are enough possibilities. Kramer, the people Cogen scammed, Rosemarie, someone from the Disciples. You're just going to get a headache trying to guess the killer. Me, I'm going home, sip a glass of an excellent Oregon pinot noir to celebrate, and soak in a tub filled with steaming-hot water. See you in the morning."

PART SIX

STARLIGHT

CHAPTER FORTY-SIX

Muriel Lujack's caseload was back to normal as soon as Billy Kramer's death had relieved her of the responsibility of handling a murder case. Her week had been one of her easiest because all her cases had ended with plea deals.

Muriel had an armed robbery case that looked like it would go to trial at the end of the following week, but she was up to speed on it, and she was looking forward to hiking a trail on the Oregon coast on the weekend.

On Thursday, Muriel knocked off work early and read until seven before turning on her television to the channel that showed classic movies. *Citizen Kane* was on her top ten all-time movie list, and she watched it for the umpteenth time. When it was over, she got into bed. She had just shut her eyes when a sudden thought made her sit up, eyes wide open.

What was Rosebud in *Citizen Kane*? That was the central mystery in the movie, and it turned out to be a sled. What was Starlight? Muriel thought she might know the answer. She got out of bed and booted up her laptop. An hour later, she knew she was right.

"I think I know who the DA is," Muriel said as soon as Karen joined her in a booth in the back of the restaurant in Sandy where they had met before. "I watched *Citizen Kane* last night. Have you seen it?"

"Years ago."

"Do you know what *Rosebud* was in the movie?"

Karen's brow furrowed. Then she remembered. "Isn't it the name of a sled?"

"Right. It's the trade name of the sled Kane was playing on when he was a child on the day he was taken from his home and his mother."

"What's that got to do with finding the traitor in your office?"

"*Rosebud* was a thing. I started wondering if *Starlight* was a thing. And it is. I remembered that one of our DAs lives on a sailboat. Owners of large boats have to register them. I called the Coast Guard. *Starlight* is the name of an Island Packet 380, an oceangoing sailboat. It's the Mercedes-Benz of sailboats. It sells for two hundred thousand dollars. In other words, it's expensive to buy, and there are other expenses, like the cost of keeping it in the marina and fuel. Ellen Kaufman makes a DA's salary, but she lives on an Island Packet 380 named *Starlight*."

Karen looked sick. "Ah, no. I really like Ellen."

"I do too, but there's more. Once I had the name, I started going back over any cases that involved the Disciples. Ellen only handled a few, but she lost some she should have won, and she assigned Donna Ridley to some cases where evidence was misplaced or legal errors led to a dismissal. There weren't many cases like that, and there were guilty verdicts—mostly for minor offenses that led to probation or a short sentence—but there were enough to form a pattern.

"As soon as I knew about the boat, I researched Ellen's background. She's local. Her family isn't rich, and she went to a public high school. I got her high school yearbook. She went to the same high school Walter Zegda attended. They were in the same grade. She was also a cop before she was a DA, and she was on a SWAT team, which means she has the skills with a rifle to take out Walter Zegda."

"You've gone way out of your way to help me, Muriel. I can't even begin to thank you."

"What are you going to do?"

"I don't know. From what you've told me, there's no hard evidence that would lead to an indictment."

"It's all circumstantial, and it rests on Raymond Castor's statement, which a good defense attorney would have no trouble calling into question."

Karen put her hand over Muriel's. "There is something I want you to promise me."

"What's that?"

"You have to back away from this and let me handle it from now on. If Ellen is the traitor in the DA's office, she is incredibly dangerous. If she suspects that you are involved in outing her, she might have no qualms about killing you."

"You don't have to scare me to get me to drop out."

"Good. And please know that I owe you a debt. Anytime you think I can help you, never hesitate to ask."

"I didn't do this for a reward."

"I know. That's why you have earned my undying respect."

Karen had a hard time concentrating when she drove home. She couldn't be certain that Ellen had betrayed her, but it was starting to look that way. Something else occurred to her. If she was the person who tried to kill Walt Zegda, she hadn't tried to kill him to cover up a connection to Terrance Cogen's scams. She'd probably done the deed to prevent Zegda from making a plea deal that forced him to identify the traitor in the DA's office, if he was arrested in connection with Cogen's scams.

The person Thomas Horan saw in the mirror had long, black hair, and so did Kaufman. In fact, Kaufman and Rosemarie Cogen were similar in height, build, and the way they wore their hair. Did Kaufman kill Cogen to protect Walt Zegda?

Karen was too tired to work out answers to the questions her meeting with Muriel had raised. She would need a clear head for that and a lot of help.

CHAPTER FORTY-SEVEN

One month after Karen's meeting with Muriel Lujack, Morris Johnson was watching the marina where the *Starlight* was docked. At six in the evening, Ellen Kaufman boarded her, and Morris called his boss. When Karen arrived, Kaufman was sitting on the deck, drinking a beer and watching the sun set.

"Nice boat," Karen said.

Kaufman smiled. "Hey, Karen, Morris. What are you doing down here? I don't have any cases with you, do I?"

"No cases," Karen said. "But we do have business to discuss."

"What business?" Kaufman asked as the lawyer and her investigator boarded the sailboat.

"This is a terrific boat. I'm thinking of buying one. I bet it cost a fortune," Karen said.

"It ain't cheap."

"What's it going for new?"

"About two hundred, but you can get them for less if the owner wants to sell."

"Did Walt Zegda help you buy this beauty?"

Ellen stopped smiling. "Why would you ask me that?"

"Just before he died, Morris asked Ray Castor for the name of the DA who was Walt Zegda's mole. He didn't say a name, but he did say *Starlight*. It took a while to figure out what that meant, but as soon as I learned the name of your boat and the fact that you've known Zegda since high school, I started to dig."

"When you're as rich as I am, you can hire the best people. That's what I did. Before I came here, I left a report compiled by a team of forensic accountants with the US attorney. It details your offshore bank accounts and syncs deposits with accounts controlled by Mr. Zegda. The report makes fascinating reading. It also mentions that you are an expert with a rifle and would have had no trouble shooting Mr. Zegda so he couldn't out you if he was arrested."

Kaufman looked stunned. "Why did you do that?" she asked.

"What would you do if someone framed you for a crime you didn't commit, was responsible for getting you disbarred, and made you spend a year in prison? Would you forgive them, or would you return the favor? I'm a firm believer in an eye for an eye, Ellen. I want you living in a dirty, airless cell where you'll never be able to see the sunset and where each day will be pure hell."

Kaufman stood up. "You bitch."

"Easy, Ellen," Morris said as he moved his jacket aside so Kaufman could see his gun.

Kaufman froze.

"I am a bitch," Karen said. "And you're going to find out just how big a bitch I am."

Kaufman started to perspire. "Look, Karen, I have information I can trade. I know who murdered Terrance Cogen."

"What do you know about Cogen?"

"I know he was too stupid to think up the scams he pulled, and I know Zegda worked with the person who manipulated Cogen and knows where the money is hidden."

"Who is it?"

"One of the few people who is smarter than Walter Zegda, and there aren't very many people who are."

"You're talking about Rosemarie Cogen?"

"Maybe."

"How do you know this?"

"I know Zegda was working Terrance Cogen's scams with her. I've read the investigative reports on Cogen. He was a lightweight, and he was going to be arrested. He would have given up his wife and Zegda in a heartbeat. That's why his wife had to kill him."

"And I didn't try to kill Walt. She did."

"Do you have any hard evidence that proves Rosemarie Cogen killed her husband and tried to kill Zegda?"

"If I do, I'm not turning it over without a deal."

Kaufman stopped talking and looked at the end of the pier. Audrey Packer and Chad Remington were walking toward her accompanied by several uniformed officers.

Kaufman stared for a moment. Then she sat down and finished her beer.

"I hope that tasted great, Ellen," Karen said, "because it's the last beer you're going to drink for a long time."

CHAPTER FORTY-EIGHT

It was almost ten in the evening, and Chad Remington, Audrey Packer, Morris Johnson, and Karen Wyatt were sitting in a booth in a tavern near police headquarters where they had agreed to meet after Ellen Kaufman had been booked and interrogated.

"Houston, we have a problem," Remington said. "We have two women who resemble each other so much that they both could have been the person Horan saw in the mirror. And they both have a motive to kill Terrance Cogen and Walter Zegda."

"Let's not forget that it's possible that one of the ladies killed Cogen and the other one tried to shoot Zegda, and vice versa," Karen said.

"This is giving me a headache," Audrey said.

"My money is on Rosemarie for the Cogen murder," Chad said.

"Why?" Morris Johnson asked.

"It's the milkshake. Ellen swears that she can't remember ever meeting Terrance Cogen, and with the exception of what she read about his murder and what she knew about the investigation into his schemes, she didn't know anything about him. She also says that she doesn't remember ever being in Dunthorpe."

"I agree," Audrey said. "Ellen doesn't run in Cogen's social circle, so how would she know about Cogen's addiction to his milkshakes? And even if she did, how would she get Cogen in a social situation where she could dope his drink?

"And another thing. Kaufman is strong, and she trained as a cop. Cogen was a wimp, from what we've heard. She would have been able to overpower him without a weapon, but she owns a handgun and could have gotten the best of him that way, so why would she resort to poisoning his drink?"

"We know Zegda thinks Rosemarie tried to kill him. Has he said anything that helps us figure out who did what?" Karen asked.

"No. He hasn't said a word since he asked to speak to his lawyer."

"Billy Kramer said that he saw a car leaving the area around Cogen's estate. Do we have anything on it?"

"It does show up on CCTV footage, but you can't see the license plate or identify the make."

"Do we have anything you can use to arrest Rosemarie?" Karen asked.

"Not a thing. All the evidence is circumstantial," Chad said.

"You should sic your forensic accountants on her," Audrey told Karen.

"Why don't you use your people?" Karen asked.

"Frank Curtin nixed it. He said he'd authorize the use of our manpower if we could give him evidence that supports an investigation. He's afraid that the press would eat us alive if they found out we were going after the widow of a murder victim who is the terrified kidnap victim of a vicious gang leader."

"So, we're at a dead end," Morris said.

"It's early days," Chad said. "We just have to keep digging. If Rosemarie is the bad guy, something will show up."

"From your lips to God's ears," Karen said.

Half an hour later, the party broke up.

"Are you doing anything interesting over the weekend?" Karen asked as she and Johnson walked to their cars.

"Vera and I are taking the kids to the Maryhill Museum."

Karen frowned. "I think I've heard of it. Isn't it out on the Columbia River Gorge on the Washington side?"

Morris nodded. "You should go. It's pretty unique, and it's got an odd history."

"Oh?"

"The museum was originally intended as a mansion for Sam Hill and his wife, Mary, the daughter of James J. Hill, a Great Northern Railroad baron. He started building it in the early 1900s as the centerpiece of an Eden-like agricultural community on the gorge, but he had to abandon his plan when he found out that the land was too arid to get enough water for farming. The construction was halted when World War I started, and it was dedicated as a museum in 1926 by Queen Marie of Romania. What's cool is that Maryhill has a really diverse collection. There are American and European paintings, works by Auguste Rodin, three hundred chess sets from around the world, and American Indian beadwork and baskets. There's even a replica of Stonehenge nearby. And the setting is great."

"It sounds interesting."

"It is definitely worth the trip. How about you? Anything going on this weekend?"

Karen blushed. "I've been seeing Barry Clay."

"The expert witness?"

"Yeah."

"He seems like a nice guy."

"He is. We're going out to the coast on Saturday."

"I'm glad to hear you're seeing someone. It's about time you started getting out there."

Karen sighed. "It has been a while."

"Don't worry. It's just like riding a bicycle. Even if you haven't done it for a while, you remember how to keep your balance pretty quickly."

It was a little after eleven when Karen walked into the living room in her penthouse and looked out at the lights of the city. She had discovered the person who had betrayed her and her quest for revenge was finally over. She had ended one chapter in her life, and she felt as if she was starting another.

Karen smiled. Barry Clay had booked a room at a hotel on the beach with an ocean view. Karen had checked. The room had one king-size bed. She knew what that meant. She hadn't slept with a man since before her legal troubles started more than two years earlier. She really liked Barry, and she was ready to see if the relationship would work, but she was nervous, and she hoped that Morris was right about riding a bicycle.

The excitement of the arrest had worn off, and Karen felt drained. She got ready for bed and turned off the lights. She was starting to drift off when she remembered something Morris had said. Karen opened her eyes. What was it? Something about the Maryhill Museum . . .

"Rodin!" Karen sat up in bed and stared at the wall. Then she got out of bed and grabbed her phone.

"Morris," she said when her investigator answered. "I want

you to write down everything you remember about what Rosemarie Cogen said at the Westmont when I asked her if anything valuable had been stolen from the Dunthorpe place."

"I don't have to remember what she said. It spooks people if you take out a pen and write down what they're saying during an interview, so I leave my phone on in my pocket and record the conversation. I've got Rosemarie live."

CHAPTER FORTY-NINE

"Thanks for meeting with us," Chad Remington said when Rosemarie Cogen let him and Audrey Packer into her penthouse.

"You said this was about prosecuting Walter Zegda for kidnapping me."

"Right. He'll probably plead, but unfortunately, we need to go over what happened in case he decides to go to trial."

The detectives followed Rosemarie into the living room. Aaron Jessup got up from the couch.

"I hope you don't mind that I asked Aaron to sit in?" Rosemarie said.

"Hi, Aaron," Chad said.

"So, what do you want to know?" Rosemarie asked when they were all seated.

For the next half hour, Rosemarie told the detectives about

the kidnapping and her encounter with Walter Zegda and Gabby Wright.

"We will have to call you to testify, if Zegda elects to go to trial. Are you okay with that?" Chad asked.

"I'm not going to enjoy seeing that monster again, but I will testify."

"Thanks. We know how stressful it's going to be, and we appreciate your willingness to help us put Zegda away so he can't hurt anyone else," Chad said.

"Say, have you been back to your Dunthorpe place since Mr. Cogen was killed?" Audrey asked.

"Why do you want to know?"

"It's something that came up. The case is still open. I've been told that there are a lot of valuable paintings, jewelry, and art objects in the house. We're trying to see if Mr. Cogen could have been killed by a robber."

"I went through the house with my insurance agent."

"When was that?"

"A week ago. The valuable paintings and art objects are insured. He had a list. Everything, including my jewelry, was still there."

"That's good to know," Chad said. "Have you had a chance to look at any of the reports in your husband's case?"

Rosemarie looked confused. "What kind of reports?"

"Police reports, the autopsy report, any other official documents?"

"How would I see them? No."

"I've been told that Karen Wyatt and her investigator talked to you at the Westmont Country Club."

"That's right. She also wanted to know if anything valuable had been stolen from the mansion."

Chad chuckled. "Did you tell her that your husband was killed with Rodin's *The Thinker*, but the killer wouldn't have taken it, because it was covered with blood and he wouldn't be able to sell it?"

Rosemarie grimaced. "I shouldn't have made that joke. It was really in bad taste."

"I agree," Audrey said. "But how did you know that Mr. Cogen had been beaten to death with *The Thinker*?"

Rosemarie frowned. "I . . . It was in the paper. He was bludgeoned to death with a marble statue."

"We've read every newspaper account and watched all of the stories on TV. None of them identify the statue that was used."

"*The Thinker* was evidence at the trial," Rosemarie said. "We saw it wasn't in the house when I went there with the insurance agent."

"Both of those times were well after Miss Wyatt talked to you."

"Where is this going, Chad?" Aaron Jessup asked.

"There are several statues in the room where Terrance Cogen was killed. The only way your client could know which statue the killer used is if she was the one who killed him."

CHAPTER FIFTY

Thomas Horan woke up from a deep, peaceful sleep. He had not had a nightmare for a while, and the few dreams he had experienced in the past few weeks had not left him terrified and exhausted.

Horan was usually up before the sun, but today, he had slept past seven. He got out of bed quietly so as not to disturb Francine and went into the bathroom. Thomas was certain that the disappearance of his nightmares was the result of the reappearance of his memories of the night Terrance Cogen died. The memories had returned slowly and they made him sad, because Terrance was his oldest friend.

On the night Rosemarie killed her husband, Terrance called his friend and told him that his lawyer had warned him that criminal charges were imminent. Then he had begged his friend for help. Thomas knew that he would not be able to help. He had skirted the law on occasion, but he had never crossed the line. If Terrance had, he would have to face the consequences.

Thomas dreaded going to Terrance's home and telling Terrance that he would not try to influence the outcome of an investigation. But he knew he had to go to provide comfort for his friend, who had always stood by him.

Horan still did not have a clear memory of the events at the house, but Rosemarie had probably given her husband the doctored milkshake after he'd made the call and had killed him shortly before Horan entered the house. It was a brutal way for Terrance's life to end, but maybe a quick end was better than the public humiliation of a trial and years in prison.

When Thomas started to shave, he looked in the mirror. Who was the man he saw there? The latest polls showed him with a significant lead over his opponent, but the lead did not excite him the way it had in the past. He had managed to sidestep and finesse questions about his claim of an alien abduction, but he knew that there would come a time when he would have to face them head-on and admit that he had never been a prisoner of visitors from another planet. He wondered if that would mark the end of his political career and whether he would care. Winning had always been so important before. Now he wondered if winning was worth it. When he told Francine about his doubts, she reminded him of how important his work was for the people he represented in Congress. Being a lawmaker did matter, but his ordeal had made him think about other ways he might make a difference.

When Thomas returned to the bedroom, Francine was getting dressed to drive him to the airport for his trip to DC.

"Did you sleep okay?" she asked. In the past, that had just been a nice question to ask a spouse. Since his ordeal, it was an important thing to know.

"Yeah, honey, I slept great." He smiled and hugged his wife. "I think the worst is over."

And he truly believed that the trauma that had ravaged him was in the past. But the aftermath had left him with questions about who he was and what he wanted to be. He could only hope that he would make the best choices.

CHAPTER FIFTY-ONE

Karen Wyatt walked onto the deck of her second-floor hotel room and stared at the massive rocks that jutted out of the ocean. The tide was coming in, and waves were crashing against the rocks, spraying foam into the air before gravity pulled the waves down and sent them racing up the beach. The white noise was calming and in tune with the peace she was feeling for the first time in a long time.

Barry was taking a shower. They'd made love again when they woke up, and it had been better than the first time when she'd been nervous and hesitant. She'd told Barry that she hadn't made love in years, and he'd been considerate and patient. This morning, he didn't have to be. Morris was right about the bicycle analogy.

Karen smiled. After all those years in hell, the universe was back in balance. Jack Blackburn had a job Karen had arranged at a garage owned by a client whose case she had won. The polls showed that Thomas Horan had a commanding lead on his opponent. Just before she'd left for the coast, Audrey Packer had called to tell her that Rosemarie Cogen was under arrest and to thank her for the recording of the conversation with Rosemarie at the Westmont and her deduction about the Rodin sculpture. Earlier in the week, she'd learned that Ellen Kaufman was going to accept a plea offer that would send her to the same prison where Karen had suffered.

The only bad news was that Frank Curtin had promoted Oscar Vanderlasky to the position of chief criminal deputy. Although that news might not be all bad. It was always better to go up against a vain and incompetent DA than one like Muriel Lujack.

Karen heard the bathroom door open, and Barry walked out. They were going to walk into town to eat at a breakfast spot Barry knew.

"Ready?" he asked.

Karen smiled. If the universe was back in balance, her life was ready to restart, and this weekend was turning into a great beginning for a new chapter.

CHAPTER FIFTY-TWO

The first months at Coffee Creek Correctional Facility, Oregon's women's prison, hadn't gone too badly. Rosemarie had to bunk with another inmate, but her cellmate was in for a nonviolent crime, and they were getting along. The cell wasn't spacious, but it had a toilet and a desk, and she was adjusting.

The prosecutors had agreed to drop the murder charge in exchange for a plea to manslaughter and the return of the money she and Terrance had stolen. Aaron Jessup thought she'd be out in five years if she was a model prisoner.

The authorities had located most of the offshore accounts, but they had missed a few, and Rosemarie hadn't volunteered the location of the nest eggs she would tap when she was free. Even if the cops found the other accounts, Rosemarie wasn't worried about money. She was a whiz at working the market. She'd done it before, and she was confident that she could do it again.

Rosemarie had worried that Walt would seek revenge now that he knew that she'd killed Wolf Larson and tried to kill him, but he was miles away in a federal maximum-security prison, and the Disciples were in disarray, so she felt safe. Rosemarie's biggest problem was boredom. She was working in the kitchen, and there wasn't much mental stimulation from the work or the conversations with her fellow prisoners. Today, her workday had ended, and she headed back to her cell. She was reading a book about physics that was very challenging, and she wanted to get back to it before she had to go to the dining hall for dinner. She entered her cell and started to look at the desk where the book was resting, but something on her bunk caught her eye. Rosemarie walked to the bed. She saw what was on her bunk, and she started to feel faint.

"Hey, is that a Rubik's Cube?" asked her cellmate.

ACKNOWLEDGMENTS

The United States Senate held hearings on the existence of unidentified flying objects around the time I got the idea for *False Witness*, so I decided to create a character who honestly believed that he had been abducted by aliens. I asked Loots Margolin, my teenage grandson, if he would try to find out why someone would believe he was abducted by aliens and he came up with the research I used in *False Witness*. I could not have written the book without him.

Every time I write a book for Minotaur Books, I thank all of the people at the publisher who help produce the book you are reading. I don't do this to be polite. My first drafts are never fit for publication. It takes getting beaten, up by my brilliant editor, Keith Kahla, to get a draft to the point where I am proud to let you read my latest. Then there is the cover and publicity and everything else that goes into making a finished product. So, thank you Keith, Grace Gay, Rob Grom, Hector DeJean, Martin Quinn, Omar Chapa, Alisa Trager, Kenneth J. Silver, David Rotstein, Chrissy Farrell, Emma Paige West, and Isabella Narvaez.

St. Martin's wouldn't have seen *False Witness* if Jennifer Weltz, my brilliant agent, had not found a home for my books there. So, thanks again to Jennifer, Ariana Philips, Cole Hildebrand, and Ben Roy at the Jean V. Naggar Literary Agency.

Finally, I want to thank Melanie Nelson, my fabulous wife, who makes my life a nonstop adventure, and Daniel, Ami, Amanda, Loots, and Marissa Margolin and Peter Watts for their continuous support.

ABOUT THE AUTHOR

Anthony Georgis

Phillip Margolin is the author of over twenty-five novels, many of them *New York Times* bestsellers, including *Gone, But Not Forgotten* and *The Third Victim*. Margolin was also a prominent criminal defense attorney for many years. He lives in Portland, Oregon.